The Catnip Caper

Professor Higgins Investigates-2

Victoria LK Williams

June 2023

CATNIP CAPER

First edition. July 1, 2023.

Copyright © 2023 Victoria LK Williams.

ISBN: 979-8215064887

Written by Victoria LK Williams.

Table of Contents

Professor Higgins Investigates - 2

Catnip Caper

Victoria LK Williams

Chapter 1

H arry raced upstairs ahead of Lizzie and Trisha, eager to chase whatever dust bunnies he could find swirling around in the morning sunlight that came through the oversized windows on either side of the enormous fireplace.

"What's he in such a hurry for? Does he have a date with the family ghost?" Trisha let Harry pass her, not wanting to be tripped, laughing as she spoke, her short dark hair bobbing with the movement of her head.

"Harry has his own agenda. And our resident ghost? She has hers as well. In fact, I haven't seen her since we started moving all these boxes in." Lizzie joined her in laughter and hurried up the last few steps to catch up with Harry. Who knew what kind of trouble he could get into with all the boxes that were stacked on the mezzanine floor? When they reached the top step, Trisha put her hands on her hips and looked around in astonishment.

"Geez, Lizzie, what did you do? Bring the entire college library here? Is there even going to be room for the furniture we picked out with all these books?"

"Oh, stop your complaining. It's not as bad as it looks. Once we put these books on the shelves, there will be plenty of room. Just be thankful we didn't have to carry all these boxes up the stairs."

"No, we can thank Mrs. Meadows for that. I think she was eager to get rid of all the books you had all over the place at the main house, plus the boxes you'd brought back from your office at the college. What do you need all these for, anyway? You're retired now."

There was a moment of silence, a guilty silence that Trisha recognized immediately. They had known each other since they were children. She knew her best friend as well as she knew herself. Trisha turned her stare from the boxes to the woman standing beside her and didn't blink, waiting for an explanation.

"About that retirement... It might have to be semiretired for a while."

"Oh, Lizzie, you promised you were done."

"And technically I am." She sighed deeply and quickly explained, hoping to wipe away her friend's disapproval, "The chancellor asked me to come back just as a consultant until they could find a replacement to take over the horticulture program at the college. Things kind of fell through when my replacement was murdered. Especially when it was the next person in line after her who committed the murder. I couldn't leave Russel Mallery hanging. Not after I'd poured my heart and soul into that program for so long."

Trisha didn't answer immediately, thinking back to the murder the two of them had been involved in solving. Then she thought of something else, "And what does Kevin have to say about this?"

"Well, I haven't come right out and told him. I mean, he knows that I've been taking phone calls from the chancellor and going over to the college periodically, but I don't think he—"

"Oh, don't worry about that; Kevin's probably got this figured out even before you did. But it is temporary, right?"

"Absolutely. I've got more than enough things to keep me busy here at Azalea Plantation. And you've got quite the list going for me on this renovation filming."

As she spoke, Lizzie waved her hands around her to emphasize the work ahead of her, and Trisha grinned back at her.

"It's fun—admit it. And you're loving every minute of this renovation, aren't you?"

Lizzie shared Trisha's grin, and gave a nod, but Harry quickly diverted their attention by clawing at one box, eager to get inside.

"Come on, let's get to work. The sooner we're done, the sooner we can go out and decide exactly where we're filming this afternoon's segment." Lizzie stepped forward and shooed Harry off the box so she could begin emptying it.

Trisha followed suit, and after a moment, they were busy breaking the seals on the boxes so they could begin placing the books on the shelves. Trisha knew better than to place a book herself. Lizzie would have a specific area for each book, and it made no sense to do double work. She motioned Lizzie toward the shelves and passed the books to her friend for Lizzie to put them on the shelf.

They worked steadily for half an hour, chitchatting about nothing in particular. Then they heard the sounds of the kitchen door opening and heard a woman's voice yelling a morning greeting. Before Lizzie could return the greeting, there was the sound of a crash, and Trisha and Lizzie turned to head down the stairs to make sure everything was okay. But the woman's voice stopped them in their tracks.

"Be more careful with those boxes. She hasn't even moved in yet, and you're already breaking things."

"Oops, somebody's getting Nora's wrath," Trisha looked over at Lizzie and grinned. "Glad it wasn't me."

The two women burst into laughter and a few moments later, they could hear someone walking up the stairs. When the messy brown hair scattered with gray appeared, followed by the sturdy build of a woman, they called out a morning greeting to Nora Meadows, housekeeper, manager, and drill sergeant for Azalea Plantation.

"My, aren't you two up and at them early? I don't know what your rush is, Lizzie. There is no reason for you to move over here yet. You don't even have furniture. Things were fine the way they were at the bed-and-breakfast," grumbled Nora Meadows in the way of greeting.

Lizzie walked over and gave the woman a hug and a kiss on the cheek.

"We've been over this so many times, Nora. I'm underfoot over there. Besides, we're coming into the peak of tourist season, and you can use my room to rent out to guests. There is no need for a lot of furniture right this instant. I want to make sure when I get my pieces that they are perfect for the look of the house. They need to be as close to authentic as possible. For right now, a blow-up bed and a nightstand are all I need in the bedroom, and that way I'm over here while they're doing work."

Nora stared at her and slowly smiled, knowing she would not win the argument they had been having for the last several weeks. Right from the time Lizzie made the decision to renovate the old family home and make it her own, Nora understood she would move there eventually. The older woman had been stalling, hoping that it wouldn't happen so soon. Harry walked over and rubbed against her legs as she bent down and scooped the cat up, giving him a treat from the pocket of her apron.

"Well, you may not have furniture, but you are going to have a well-equipped kitchen. I'll not have you move in here without being able to fend for yourself." Scratching Harry's head, Nora attempted to have the last say.

"A coffee pot and a microwave are all I need, Nora. You know I don't cook. I'm taking my meals over at the main house with everybody else."

"Nonsense. You may as will do it right, and since the kitchen is ready, let's make it complete. Now, I came over to let you know Kevin called to say he'd be over in a couple of hours after the film crew has arrived."

"The film crew! Holy crap, I forgot about them." Trisha glanced at her watch and shoved the book she had in her hands at Lizzie.

"Thanks, Nora. I need to get downstairs and direct them where to go. Unfortunately, it's a substitute crew today, so I'm going to have to be on top of them every step of the way."

"You said nothing about a substitute crew. What happened?"

"Our usual crew had to go film a commercial on the other side of the state. It was a bit of an emergency, but they assured me the crew they have lined up to help them out will be just as good, and it's only for a week. Just this one episode."

Trish didn't stick around to explain any further. Giving Mrs. Meadows a kiss on her cheek as she rushed by, Trisha headed downstairs, her feet clumping on the old wooden floors.

"Was it my imagination, or did Trisha sound less confident than her words indicated?" Mrs. Meadow watched Trisha disappear from view and turned back to Lizzie.

"I caught her tone as well. Today could be an interesting day."

Harry seemed to agree with her assessment, and he squirmed to get out of Mrs. Meadows's arms. Jumping to the floor, he raced after Trisha, intent on being in on any action that might happen.

"I hope he stays out from underfoot when the crew gets here." Lizzie frowned as she watched him scurry down the stairs.

"Fat chance. If there's trouble to be found, Harry will be in the middle of it. Now leave those boxes and come down to the kitchen with me; there are a few things I want to show you." Mrs. Meadows's voice didn't allow for any arguments. Lizzie set the books in her hands down and took one last look around the mezzanine, which was soon to be her private library. Her eyes lingered on the stems of blooming azaleas on the mantel. They were there when she'd arrived in the morning, and she knew they were a sign of welcome. It seemed the family ghost was happy she was moving in.

Chapter 2

For the second or third time, Lizzie looked wistfully out the kitchen window, watching Trisha move quickly around the back patio, getting ready for the crew to arrive. Nora Meadows was in her glory as she showed Lizzie all the new gadgets and appliances installed in her kitchen. She could have been talking Greek for all Lizzie knew. Like she had said, she wasn't much of a cook, and she failed to understand why Nora felt it was so important for her to have a fully equipped kitchen.

But Lizzie had agreed to let Nora have free rein in this area when they had started the renovations of the old house. The main plantation house was Nora's domain, and when Lizzie had needed a project when she retired, the original family homestead was the perfect solution.

She was surprised to find the interior of the house was in such good condition. There was no dry rot, no sagging ceilings or buckling floors. There was plenty of dirt and cobwebs and lizards, much to Harry's delight, and they found the house merely needed to be modernized rather than gutted and brought up to code. The broad wooden staircase that led to the second floor was structurally sound, and when they started stripping the floors, they found beautiful wood underneath.

The mezzanine, which Lizzie had claimed for her library, overlooked the first floor with a beautiful hand-carved railing. An enormous fireplace took up much of the outer wall, connecting to the fireplace below in the living room.

There were four bedrooms on the second floor, but they were small, and Lizzie had quickly hired a contractor to design two suites on the second floor, combining the four rooms into two, one on either side of the mezzanine.

The downstairs had a huge Florida room with large sliding windows that opened up to allow a cross breeze to enter. Once it was rescreened, Lizzie had claimed this area as an office/sitting room. The main living room would be for entertaining, and she had eliminated the formal dining room, making the two rooms into one. She had a great time with Trisha shopping in second-hand stores and vintage stores to find the perfect furniture, which was soon to be delivered. She was determined to keep the feeling of the old house. This had been the one stipulation she had told Nora; she could do whatever she wanted, but it had to have an old country look to it. She wanted nothing that glared modern.

"Lizzie, are you even paying any attention to me?" Nora's frustrated voice made Lizzie smile, and she honestly shook her head.

"I told you, Nora, show me where the coffee pot and the microwave are, and I'm good to go. Not that I don't appreciate all the effort you put in. This is gorgeous, and I love the plates and old-fashioned pots and pans that you bought. These cast-iron frying pans are wonderful."

"I know you don't think you're going to be cooking, but eventually trudging across the yard and around the pond to come get every meal is going to get old. And I'm sure you're going to want to entertain. Don't dismiss my hard work in here so easily."

"Please don't think that's what I'm doing. I really appreciate everything you did. And you're right, of course. I'm going to have to cook some meals here. The idea of entertaining actually sounds appealing. I hope you help me when I decide to start that, Nora."

Lizzie's appeal for help with entertainment soothed the ruffled feathers Nora was developing.

"All right, I've held your attention long enough. Check out what your friend is doing out there, and remember, I don't want the film crew in here traipsing through the kitchen or any other rooms until they are properly set up." Nora waved her hands toward the door, shoving Lizzie out with a final word of warning.

"There should be no need for the film crew to be in here until we're completely finished with redecorating. They got all their before-renovation shots, and now we're going to concentrate on the gardens."

"And you will be in your glory, reworking those overgrown beds. I love the idea that you're starting with the patio and that immense fireplace. And a kitchen garden will be the perfect addition. Thank you for agreeing to that."

"It was a great idea, Nora. It won't be anywhere as big and intense as the kitchen garden off the bed-and-breakfast, but it will be sufficient, and I ordered some catnip to be planted for Harry."

"Ha! " Nora gave a short laugh, "like Harry needs catnip to get into mischief. You might regret that decision. Now go on and go." Nora turned her back away from Lizzie and opened another box to place the utensils and cutlery into the drawers.

Lizzie didn't need a second invitation, and she quickly made her escape. As she walked out onto the beautiful patio, she felt a tinge of excitement. They had deliberately left the outside renovations until last, so that they could do the filming to record their progress.

"It's a beautiful day to start this," she called out to Trisha, who was shooing Harry away from the fireplace.

When Lizzie had taken over the old house, she'd been delighted to find the fireplace was still in excellent condition, and with Kevin's help, they had discovered they did not make the patio of mere blocks of concrete. Instead, her ancestors had brought in beautiful black terrazzo slabs to create the oversize patio. The black stone was infused with tiny seashells, and when they were done with the renovations, the terrace floor would be the centerpiece. There were gardens that had been allowed to become overgrown and weed infested all around the house. During the filming of the discovery of what the old house offered, Kevin and Trisha had decided where they were going to start, and which gardens would be renovated, and which would be eliminated. It was a gigantic project, but they were excited to undertake it.

Kevin Lowe was the third part of Lizzie's trio. The three of them, Lizzie, Trisha, and Kevin, had grown up together and spent many afternoons wandering the plantation exploring. As they had grown up, they'd gone in their own direction. Lizzie moved into horticulture, teaching some classes at first, then quickly working her way up to becoming the dean of the horticulture program. Kevin had started his own publications company. Trish had developed her own skills with filmmaking and usually had several projects going. But her favorite project was Lizzie's gardening show. They filmed out at the plantation, bringing in guest speakers, covering all aspects of gardening and exotic plants and birds of Florida.

Over time, Lizzie had established research gardens on the plantation property. Students from the college worked in the gardens, and their top gardener, Josh Bedingfield, had multiple pet projects creating new combinations of flowering plants.

"So, what are we focusing on today?" Lizzie asked Trisha as she looked around.

"Right now, I'm focusing on trying to get Harry out of the way. He's right where I want to film."

"It's best to just ignore him. The harder you work at trying to move him, the more stubborn he's going to become and the more he'll want to stay. Once he thinks you're not interested, he will wander off and find something else to get into. So, the fireplace is where we're starting today?"

"Yes. I want to film this area, showing that it will be the focal point of the terrace and how you plan to use the gardens to frame it and provide a privacy backdrop. Sound okay to you?"

"Sounds like a plan. I don't know how you keep it all in your head. We had so many ideas of what we're going to film, and you do nothing in order."

"Well, I figure since we had a substitute crew, it would be best if we started on something that was fairly solid and wouldn't take a lot of maneuvering. I haven't worked with this crew before, and I don't really want them traipsing through your gardens. Since this is a focal point of the garden, we should start here."

Lizzie nodded in agreement and walked over to pick Harry up off the ledge of the fireplace. He claimed this as one of his special spots, and she didn't mind at all because, thanks to Harry, she had found a mysterious key hidden in the fireplace.

Lizzie had yet to figure out what it unlocked and frankly hadn't had the time to worry about it. But it was there in the back of her mind, and she knew at some point, she was going to search for the lock that key would open.

The sound of car doors slamming caught their attention, and they looked over toward the parking area of the plantation-now-bed-and-breakfast and saw three vans all labeled "Camille Shoots".

"Looks like the film crew is here. I'll run over and send them toward the patio."

"Trisha, have them park on the side road. It's closer to the house, and they won't have to lug their equipment so far."

"That'll work. Okay, let's get this started."

Chapter 3

L izzie watched Trisha race across the lawn, skirting the pond where two pairs of swans were gliding across the water.

"She always was a fast runner. " Lizzie smiled at the graceful movement of her old friend.

When Trisha reached the film crew, she barely looked like she was out of breath. Lizzie watched as she pointed toward the service road that led to the back entrance of what was now her home. The woman, who seemed in charge, gave a sharp nod and then tossed her keys to a young man standing near her. She waved the others in the direction Trisha had given, and then she started walking with Trisha across the lawn. Her strides were full of purpose, and she didn't seem to spare any chitchat with Trisha. As they got closer, Lizzie walked toward the edge of the patio to greet them.

The other woman's long strides had her reaching Lizzie before Trisha, and Lizzie smiled in greeting, holding out her hand to welcome the woman. It shocked Lizzie when her outstretched hand was completely ignored, and the woman walked past her to look around the patio sitting.

"Camille, this is Lizzie—"

"Yeah, yeah, the homeowner." Trisha had finally caught up and tried to introduce Lizzie to the other woman, only to be abruptly dismissed. The two friends exchanged looks, Lizzie's eyebrows rose in disdain, and Trisha's mouth hung open in shock. This was not a good start.

Camille finished her survey of the area and then turned back to Trisha.

"According to my notes, this is where you want to start the filming. Not sure I agree. Personally, I think the fireplace is overwhelming. But this is your show. I don't want bystanders in the way, so I'm afraid the homeowner will have to leave." Camille looked back at the fireplace and then started waving her hands, taking a step toward it. "And this cat has got to go. I'm not running a circus here, and I don't want animals in my way."

Trisha could almost see steam coming out of Lizzie's ears, and she hurried forward, ready to diffuse the tension before it got out of hand.

"Camille, let me introduce you to Lizzie Higgins. She's not only the homeowner, but she is also the host of the show. She will be staying." Trisha paused and looked down at the cat whose hair was standing up, his ears bent back, a sure sign of anger.

"And as for Harry, the cat stays, too. He's as much a part of the show as I am, and the viewers enjoy seeing him. Besides, chasing him away is only going to make him show up more," added Lizzie.

"Really?" The woman looked back and forth between Harry and Lizzie and gave an exasperated sigh. "Well, I will have to work with what I have."

Before either woman could say a word to her, she turned from them to give directions to the crew members who were arriving laden down with cameras and sound equipment.

"Oh, boy, this isn't a good start," Trisha muttered as she hurried over to help the cameraman, who had more than his share of equipment.

Camille was barking orders right and left, and there was very little chitchat. Lizzie watched silently, taking in the overall atmosphere of the workers. This was not a happy crew, which was unusual; most of the filming crews that had come out to do segments for the garden show had always been cheerful, chatty, and full of questions. This group looked like they were afraid to open their mouths.

"Look, I need to get set up, and then I'll have you come in and do your piece. I can cut and paste from that point. I'm going to want to take pictures of the terrace looking out from inside the house, and I'll need to walk around some gardens."

Camille had walked up to stand next to Lizzie, and as she spoke, Lizzie understood the overall feelings of her crew. She kept her mouth shut, knowing full well if she opened it, she was going to say something that would not go over well. Trisha quickly intervened.

"Sorry, Camille, filming inside the house is off-limits. I gave you directions on what we are going to be doing today, and that's it. Please don't expand on what we want to cover. We're going to leave that for our normal film crew."

The woman gave a sharp bark of laughter and turned to look at Trisha head-on.

"Listen, anybody that works with Camille Shoots doesn't go back to anybody else after working with the best. You may as will figure on not using your other crew. Besides, I know she's tied up for at least three weeks, and if you want the segments to get off on your schedule, you have to work with me. Your hands are tied."

Trisha was ready to say something, but Lizzie put a hand on her arm, forcing her to stop, and gave a slight shake of her head. There was no sense in getting into an argument before they'd even filmed the first segment. Camille was right. They were on a time schedule, and it was unfortunate that they would have to stick with her for at least one or two segments. Lizzie drew herself up into a full professor regime and took control of the situation before Trisha's temper got out of whack.

"Camille, if we're going to work together, then we're going to need to work efficiently and compatibly. We gave you complete instructions and very specific requirements. If you can't meet these, we can make other arrangements. I know of several film companies down in Orlando that would be more than happy to help me. It's in your court; are you going to follow my guidelines or pack it up and just head back out?" The other woman looked at Lizzie in surprise and then seemed to take her in, reassessing her initial opinion. A haughty smile crossed her face, and she gave a slight bow of her head.

"I can compromise. I have your instructions, but I don't take any interference in my filming."

"Just remember. I have the final say of anything that gets put together for the show. You remember that, and things will work out fine." Lizzie turned on her heel and walked away from the woman, leaving Trisha to deal with her.

Harry jumped down from the fireplace and followed her as she walked across the patio to help Camille's assistant, who was struggling with a large box.

"Here, let me help you with that." She reached out to grab a corner of the box to balance it better for the young girl, smiling reassuringly. It was obvious everybody was a little afraid of Camille.

"Thank you, it was a little heavier than I thought," the soft voice answered, and Lizzie caught the slight southern accent. It was more pronounced than even Trisha's, and she looked at the girl with interest.

She had dyed her hair bright pink, and Lizzie wondered if it was in defiance or a lark. Dressed in traditional cutoff jeans and a T-shirt. Underneath the bright pink hair, her skin glowed with youth. Too much youth, Lizzie thought. She doesn't look old enough to be working on a film crew full-time. Maybe as an after-school job, and she wondered what the girl's parents thought of her working in such tense conditions. Or did they even know?

"I'm Lizzie Higgins. If you need anything, let me know. I've already put a large cooler of soda and water over in the shade for you guys, so help yourselves, and the restrooms are right off the kitchen."

"Great, nice to know those things from the beginning. Oh, my name is Kelly Sky. This is a beautiful place, and I'm looking forward to filming here."

"Kelly! A little less chitchat and a little more work. There are still things in the truck that need to come off."

Camille's voice cut across the patio, and Kelly seemed to shrink into herself, her smile fading. With a slight wave, she fled from Lizzie's side and raced back to the truck to continue unloading. Lizzie turned back toward Camille with a frown.

"This is going to be the longest segment we've ever filmed." She grumbled to herself.

But her frown quickly turned to a smile that she had to put her hand over her mouth to hide. Harry was up to no good. It was clear he knew Camille didn't like him, and he was going to cause trouble. She just knew it.

Right now, he was following the woman so closely that if she had taken a step backwards, she would've tripped right over him. But he seemed to know just when she was going to turn and hurried to get out of her line of vision, jumping up on a pile of boxes close by. When the woman turned back around, she was almost face-to-face with the cat, and his appearance made her jump in surprise.

"I want this cat outta here!"

It tempted Lizzie to run forward and rescue Camille from Harry. Not the other way around. Harry could handle himself. But then she figured, no, let Camille come to terms with Harry. One of them would win control, and she'd place money on Harry.

Chapter 4

When Kevin Lowe arrived at Azalea Plantation, he parked in the guest parking lot and made his way into the kitchen area. His stomach grumbled in anticipation; he knew there was always food for any hungry soul who wandered into the chef's domain, and he had skipped breakfast in order to get everything ready for today.

"Morning, Kevin," called out the chef in greeting as Kevin grabbed a bagel and a handful of grapes. "Everyone's over at the little plantation house."

"Even Nora?"

"Yep, she's on a mission to make sure Lizzie has a kitchen that would equal mine. Don't know why, since that women can't even scramble an egg." The two men shared a laugh at Lizzie's expense, and then the chef turned back to his souffle he was working on. Kevin headed out the kitchen door and cut across to Lizzie's house, what they were now calling the Higgins House.

As he walked across the lawn, he noticed the film crew's vans parked over on the service road, and he gave a groan. He'd hoped to be there before Camille and her crew arrived. When he had heard that Trisha had hired them as a substitute film crew, he prepared himself for any disaster possible. The most immediate one that he could think of was Lizzie and Camille squaring off with each other over control of the shoot.

"I hope Trisha's got this under control," he muttered to himself and picked up his pace to walk to the house. Rather than walking around the outside, he cut through, and he raced to the steps to the front entrance. They had refurbished the porch with fresh wood, matching the old as closely as possible. The porch was now as sturdy as when it had been originally built, and there was no danger of anybody falling through the planks. Lizzie had brought over some of the wicker chairs that sat on the patio of the unused cabins, and they lined the front porch so that she could look over the pond toward the main house.

As Kevin looked toward the guest cottages, he saw a young woman emerge from the very last one and raised his hand in greeting. The young woman saw him and returned the greeting with a wide smile. Kevin waited for her and sat down on the rocking chairs, enjoying the morning breeze and watching the figure approach. Emma Cassidy was a bright young woman who was doing an internship with his company. She was staying as a guest at the plantation through family ties. What had started out as just a month's intern had extended itself, and Kevin secretly hoped he could find a permanent position for her in the company. But he had a feeling that would not work out; Emma was getting itchy feet, giving signs of wanting to return to her hometown of Citrus Beach.

"Morning, Kevin. Are you waiting for me, or are you afraid to go face the firing squad?" Emma laughed as she reached the porch, and judging from the look on Kevin's face, this was exactly what he was thinking.

"Well, I'm hoping I got here late enough that Trisha has defused any problems."

"You're optimistic. I met Camille twice in the office. There's no getting that woman to back down. She's going to push Lizzie just so far, and ka-boom!"

"Yeah, I'm afraid it's going to be a long day until the pecking order is determined."

Emma looked at her boss and smiled, feeling sorry for him. "Anything in particular you want me to concentrate on?"

"I don't think there's much we can do about the conflict there's bound to be between Lizzie and Camille. They'll have to work that out themselves, but maybe you can help with Camille's assistant. I've seen the way she treats her staff. Maybe if we make it easier for them, the day will go smoother."

"You got it. Keep Camille focused on Lizzie and let everybody else do their jobs. Is that what you're saying?"

Kevin laughed at the look Emma was giving him. "Yep, that's exactly what I'm saying. Well, I guess we've put this off long enough. Let's see what we're up against."

Kevin held the door open for Emma, and she preceded him in a walk through the main hallway, past the grand stairway, and down a smaller hallway toward the kitchen. They both greeted Nora as they walked through, but she just waved. She was busy instructing a helper where the next load of boxes was to go. It seemed everybody was occupied with their own jobs. Kevin walked to the screen door of the kitchen and looked out onto the patio.

The sight in front of him spelled trouble. The three women he'd been trying to keep apart were standing in a semicircle, staring at each other. Lizzie had her arms crossed over her chest, Trisha was waving her hands, and Camille stood with her hands on her hips, shaking her head in disagreement.

"Here goes," Kevin muttered to himself as he stepped out onto the patio.

IT HAD TAKEN SOME DOING, but there was finally some order, and filming was finally taking place. Kevin breathed a sigh of relief and allowed himself to relax. Watching the crew work, he noted the differences between the crew members Camille had brought with her. For such a small shoot, it surprised him at the number of crew members she had with her. And they seemed like an odd match. The only thing he could see they had in common was varying degrees of fear of Camille.

Emma was doing her best to keep everybody happy, making sure that cameras had a place to be set when not in use. They had put charging stations up for laptops and computers, and everybody was supplied with cold drinks. Kevin noticed she had a warm smile for each member of the crew and an easy way of getting them to talk. She especially seemed taken with the youngest member of the crew, the girl with pink hair. Kevin noted they seemed closest in age to all those on the patio, and with a jolt, he realized she hadn't been around very many people her own age since the start of her internship.

Camille's raised voice drew his attention away from the two youngest workers on the patio, and he glanced over to see the woman waving her arms as she talked to another woman.

"Really, Ophelia, I don't know how difficult it can be to get this right. How long have you been working for me? You should know my system by now, there are no excuses—get it done!" Slapping the paper she held her hands against her thigh, Camille shook her head walked away from her assistant.

The two women couldn't be more different in appearance if they tried. Camille had the stature of a woman in control, with self-assurance and style. Her curly hair was cut in a structured bob that showed off her high cheekbones.

Her added height emphasized her athletic body. She gave the appearance of being unapproachable.

The other woman, Ophelia, had long straight blonde hair that seemed to want to hide her face, almost as if she wanted to hide herself. She wasn't as physically fit as Camille, but she looked like she could hold her own, lifting the boxes needed to set up the photo shoot and keeping up with the others. She was short, and between the shortness and her long hair, it seemed easy to overlook her, and she seemed to put no effort into drawing attention to herself, fading in the background like a little field mouse.

"I'll get right on it, Camille. " Her voice was soft, and Kevin had to strain to hear what she said.

But Camille had dismissed her from her thoughts as she turned away and was zeroing in on the next person.

"She's obviously never heard the old saying 'you attract more flies with honey than vinegar.'"

Kevin turned toward the voice at his side and grinned with pleasure when he saw Lizzie had snuck up next to him.

"I'm really sorry you have to deal with this. We were definitely between a rock and a hard place. This episode is scheduled to air next week. We can't put it off any longer."

"Don't worry about it, Kevin. With Trisha here, things will go smoothly. There are going to be bumps in the road, and I'm pretty sure there are going to be some words spoken that are going to be regretted, but we'll get through it. The episode will be fantastic just like they always are. I'm just glad we don't have a guest speaker this time," Lizzie answered.

Chapter 5

Lizzie didn't wait for Kevin's response. She was too curious about the other members of the film crew, and she wanted to get to know them before she had to do her own segment. You can tell a lot about a person from the way they work, and Lizzie was an excellent observer. Many times, she had stood back and just watched her students work out their problems in the field. She was an astute reader of people's personalities, and often their actions spoke much louder than any words they could say.

Ophelia was a quiet worker, dashing back and forth to get the work done, trying as hard as she could not to become the center of attention. She'd been right in thinking the woman was mousy, and she thought of the little field mouse Harry had been halfheartedly chasing since they'd started work on the house. The little mouse made no attempt to come in the house, but Lizzie didn't think it was from fear of Harry. If anything, Harry seemed amused by the little rodent's actions. He would often just sit and stare at the mouse, letting him come up close to the point of even getting a few nibbles of Harry's food. It was as if they were developing a friendship.

The crew was young, between twenty and thirty, making Camille the oldest one that had arrived that morning. She easily had ten years on her employees and reigned like a queen. The queen of hearts, barking out orders right and left.

Kelly Sky seemed to have the role as the general gofer, running back and forth, picking up items and taking things to other crew members. Lizzie noticed that when she wasn't working, she seemed to drift toward Emma, and they could be found talking low, so as not to draw attention from Camille.

The other member was an older man, the oldest of the crew in his mid-thirties. He was good looking and assured, almost cocky. He looked like he would be the one that would be the easiest match to take on Camille if it ever came to it. But he also seemed to avoid her like the others, only interacting with Camille when it was necessary. Lizzie wandered over toward the young man, curious about what his role was. She wasn't used to so many people coming out on a shoot. It was usually just a cameraman, the director, and somebody to work the computers. But Camille's crew was larger, and as Lizzie watched, she realized they were doing the work that Camille could easily do if she had wanted to. She treated her staff like underlings, making them do the most menial tasks. Briefly, Lizzie was glad she wasn't paying by the hour for the project.

"Tony, I want a wide angle on that fireplace. Don't go in too close. And make sure that cat isn't in the frame when you film."

The man Lizzie had just been contemplating gave a nod toward Camille. He didn't answer, but he took a few steps back, away from the fireplace. With a wry expression, Lizzie noticed him take something out of his pocket and throw it in the fireplace. With a casual stride, she walked over to see what it was, but Harry beat her to it. Hiding a smile, Lizzie saw the man was deliberately giving Harry nibbles of his breakfast bagel. Harry wasn't the only one that was trying to cause trouble on the set.

"I appreciate you want to give Harry a treat, but he tends to not know when to stop, so we limit how much food he can take in. As you can see, he's quite overweight." Lizzie walked over closer to the man called Tony and spoke to him in a low voice. He looked at her wryly and gave a shrug of his shoulders.

"I don't mind sharing my bagel, especially when there's a hidden benefit of aggravation. But if you don't want me to feed your cat, that's not a problem. How old is this fireplace?"

"I'm not sure, but I know it's well over 100 years old. They built it even before the main house and used it as part of their outdoor kitchen. That would have been common to have an immense fireplace and eating area established before they built the house. They would pitch tents or wagons around the fireplace for cooking and warmth as they waited for the house to be completed. But the house was always second. Any planting for food was the first priority." Lizzie smiled at the young man as she answered, and he looked like he was ready to ask another question. He seemed interested in the history, but Camille barked out another order, cutting off his question.

"Tony, when you've got that shot of the fireplace, get some shots of the surrounding gardens. Get as many shots as you can, and then we'll voice over the hostess, explaining what she's planning for the rest of the gardens."

Lizzie's head shot up, and she stared at Camille, taking in her words. This was not how her film segments were normally shot, and she did not like the direction Camille was planning. She looked around for Trisha or Kevin, wanting to stop things before it got out of hand. It took a moment to locate Trisha. She was busy with a woman with long brown hair and large decorative earrings. Lizzie remembered this young woman being addressed as Tiffany. The name seemed to fit her. She was a beautiful woman. Her hair was pulled off her forehead, drawing attention to her intense, almond-shaped eyes. Her makeup was perfect, and her clothes stylish, not what Lizzie normally saw one of the crew wearing. She looked like she could be one of the guests that Lizzie often interviewed.

"It was nice to talk to you, Tony, but I wouldn't get too caught up in Camille's directions. They're going to change."

With that parting shot to the cameraman, Lizzie started toward Trisha, her stride purposeful. Harry jumped down from the fireplace and followed, not wanting to miss any of the action. As Lizzie walked toward Trisha, she caught Kevin's attention and made a motion for him to join them. A few moments later, the three of them were huddled in a corner by one of the large azalea bushes that gave the plantation its name, and Lizzie wasted no time expressing her displeasure.

"Look, I understand that this is a substitute crew, and there's going to be hiccups and tension. But I will not stand for her changing the way my show is filmed. She wants to do voice-overs and dubbing. It's a live gardening show! That's what my viewers want to see. Whether it's me or somebody else doing the talking, it will be live. You two better figure out how to tell Camille she needs to fulfill the contract the way it's written, not the way she interprets it."

"Come on Lizzie, it can't be that bad. She has an excellent reputation, and I've seen her work. It's good."

Kevin was the first to answer, and he tried to settle the fire in Lizzie's eyes, but his words were not working. Trisha knew Lizzie as well as a sister would, and she had to admit she was having the same feelings herself. But wanting to make sure they stayed on schedule and keep everybody happy, Trisha agreed with Kevin.

"Maybe we should see what she has planned before we go crazy. Like Kevin said, her results are always good."

"I'm not settling for just good. I want to give our viewers what they are used to, what they expect. Trisha, you of all people know the hype that you've been building over this season series on the renovations. If we don't start out on the right foot, how can recuperate as we go along? Who knows how many viewers we can lose if we don't do it right? I'm not discounting that the woman is talented, but I know my viewers, I know the guest speakers that come on, and I know the format that I've prepared for this show. I'm not deviating from what I'm used to, because it works. It's been getting us top ratings since we started."

Trisha and Kevin nodded in agreement, and they all looked in Camille's direction, watching her grab the laptop out of Tiffany's hand with a jerk.

"Which one of us is going to talk to her?"

The two women were pointing to Kevin before he finished speaking. Giving an exaggerated sigh, he started in Camille's direction.

"You two are going to owe me for this."

Trisha just laughed, but Lizzie's attention darted to the upstairs window, where the curtain was moving as if being pulled to the side by someone. But there was no one to be seen from Lizzie's vantage point. Trisha glanced over at her friend to see what had her attention and then followed her glance to the upstairs window.

"What do you see, Lizzie?"

"Nothing. But that's happened before. Stay here; I want to run upstairs for a moment."

Without waiting for a reply from Trisha, Lizzie hurried to the kitchen door. As if he knew something was about to happen, Harry raced from his spot by the fireplace and met her at the door.

"She's back, Harry," Lizzie whispered to the cat as she opened the door and slipped inside. Thankfully, Nora was busy in another room. Lizzie chased Harry up the stairs to the left suite she planned on claiming for her own.

At first glance, there was nothing out of order. Boxes were still piled, waiting for the workers to finish their final touches and the furniture to arrive. For a moment, Lizzie ignored the urge that had brought her to the room and closed her eyes to imagine what the room would look like when completed. But Harry wasn't so patient, and he meowed demandingly and jumped on a box close to the fireplace. Each of the rooms had a fireplace, something Lizzie intended to enjoy when the winter months came.

"Okay, Harry. What did you find?"

Opening her eyes, Lizzie moved to the cat's side and found him playing with a stem of azalea blossoms. Looking at the dust on the mantel, left from the construction, the words "Beware of Lies" were written in a flowing script that Lizzie recognized. Her ghostly ancestor had returned, leaving a warning.

Chapter 6

L izzie reached down and pried the azalea petals from Harry's paws. Then she looked around the room, a soft smile playing at the corner of her lips.

"Hello, Elizabeth." Lizzie whispered the greeting, not knowing if she would hear an answer or not.

As if in response, the old lace curtains hanging in the window moved like a hand waving. The window wasn't open, and there was no air movement within the room that would cause the curtains to flutter. She knew Elizabeth was responding. Her ancestor rarely showed herself, only leaving small signs like the fluttering of a curtain or some gently laid azalea blooms, often when blooming season was over.

Lizzie felt not fear, but comfort, as if her long-lost relative was looking out for her.

"What are you warning me about, Elizabeth?" Lizzie wondered out loud and walked over to the window to look down below.

As was normal when there was a shoot going on at the plantation, a small crowd had gathered. Guests from the B&B, as well as fans of the shop, seem to always know when she was shooting and showed up to watch the action. Lizzie recognized several people from town and also noticed there were a few strangers and wondered where they had come from. Her eyes swept the terrace. She could easily pick out the film crew and her friends. Several of the staff members of the research greenhouses watched the action as well, and she smiled at one of the intern's excitement. Vicki Williams was all but jumping in place, trying to see over the taller staff members in front of her. But for once, Camille was by herself, not ordering or berating anyone else. Lizzie studied the woman from the distance where she wouldn't be observed.

Camille was staring down at a piece of paper, and after looking around to see if anybody was monitoring her movements, she crumpled the paper into a ball and threw it into the fireplace. She ran her fingers through her short, cropped hair, and even from the distance, Lizzie could read her body language. The woman was mad about something, but she also seemed nervous.

"I wonder what that was all about. Come on, Harry let's go back downstairs." Lizzie paused for a moment and then spoke to the empty room, "Thanks for the message, Elizabeth. I'll be careful."

As Lizzie hurried from the room and cut across the mezzanine toward the stairway, she wondered to herself who she was promising to be careful, her ancestor or herself.

Walking back out onto the terrace, Lizzie found it was a beehive of activity. Camille's crew seemed to handle things on their own, doing what needed to be done with no instructions from her. Or at least they were not listening to her instructions, going about their routine. Lizzie couldn't help noticing that Camille was watching everyone on the set, both her employees and the spectators. Walking over to stand next to Kevin, Lizzie pointed out a man who was in his early forties. She thought for a moment, but she didn't recognize him.

"Who is that guy?"

"I think he is a film groupie. The film crew seemed to recognize him, and I heard Ophelia say hello to him by name. You know as well as I do there are always a few stalkers who come in to watch the crew working."

"You're right. There seems to be a general fascination with watching the show being put together. He sure seems to be interested in what Camille is doing, doesn't he?"

Kevin was silent for a moment as he watched Camille in action and realized Lizzie was right. The man seemed to only be watching the director.

Before Lizzie could say a word, there was a sudden argument between Camille and Tiffany. The younger woman was trying to explain that she could not do what Camille wanted with the computer program she had. But the director wouldn't listen and was growing more aggravated and louder.

"Kevin, this has to stop. I don't want the spectators to see fighting on the set." Lizzie hissed, not wanting to be overheard by anybody nearby.

She didn't have to bother telling Kevin. He agreed with her and was ready to walk over to confront the director, but Trisha beat him to it.

"Looks like I need to run some interference. Trisha's just about had it too, and it won't take much for her southern temper to flare." Without waiting for Lizzie to answer, Kevin left her side.

For a few moments, Lizzie watched Kevin and Trisha try to calm Camille down. She started looking at the people around her and noticed many were watching the confrontational trio.

She was ready to walk over when Harry wound himself around her legs and gave a soft howl. He seemed to want to tell Lizzie something and had been demanding her attention. This was the perfect chance, while everybody's focus was diverted. Swooping down, she picked up Harry. He would be a great camouflage, and she hurried over to the fireplace. Making sure she wasn't being watched, she bent over and searched inside the grate. Her goal was at the very back, and she had to stretch to reach it, but when she stood back up, Harry still in her arms, she had the crumbled ball of paper Camille had discarded. Casually walking over to the back side of the fireplace, she uncrumpled the paper and stared down at the words.

Stop your harassment before you regret it.

The words had been cut from a newspaper and pasted on the paper, like some old murder mystery. It seemed like a lot of effort to give Camille a message. And Lizzie was sure that the amateur efforts would provide some sort of clues for the police if it came to that.

Lizzie heard voices raised almost to a screaming rant, and she folded the paper up and slipped it into her pocket. She came back out around the fireplace to find Trisha closing down the shoot for the day.

"Look, sweetie, tempers are just flaring too high today. Let's all take a break. We'll start again tomorrow. You've done what you wanted to: you got a feel for the shoot, met Lizzie, and took some primary shots. Spend the rest of the day exploring and get a feel for our town. That might help you understand how we do things a little better."

"I don't think so. I'm the one who decides when we're done for the day." Camille's icy smile did nothing to warm her response to Trisha's announcement.

Lizzie drew in her breath, as if she had been punched in the stomach, and caught Kevin's glance. Camille had no idea who she was dealing with. Trisha might ooze southern charm, but when pushed, her rebel temper flared. And Camille had just pushed a little too much.

"All right everyone, we're going to call it a day. Thank y'all so much for the hard work everyone did. We'll start again tomorrow, and I'm sure things will go much smoother." She stared Camille down. "Won't they, Camille?"

The other woman sputtered, ready to argue, but looking around, she realized it would make her look like a fool if she dared. Without answering, she turned on her heel, yelling for her crew to pack it up. As she walked by Ophelia, she snatched the keys for the van the woman had been driving and left without a word, leaving Ophelia staring after her. Lizzie stepped forward, keeping Ophelia from going after her boss, deciding space needed to be put between Camille and the rest of her crew.

"You can leave your equipment here on site if that will help. In the meantime, I know the chef has a light meal set up for you down at the B&B. So help yourself and wander around the grounds before you leave. There are plenty of gardens, and it might give you a chance to see what we are planning. The Higgins house will be a smaller replica of the main plantation, and that includes the gardens. Wander around, and I'll be here if you have questions."

As the crew walked away from Lizzie, taking her up on her offer of a meal and the opportunity to explore the gardens, she couldn't help but notice their demeanor seemed much cheerier. And so did hers until she heard her name being called from the house and looked over to see a man about her own age waving his arms like a hen running around the yard, trying to get her attention.

"Oh no, not again." Lizzie groaned, not even trying to lower her voice. Kevin and Trish were standing next to her, and they turned in the direction she was looking. Both burst out laughing.

"It's not funny, you two. I should let you deal with him."

"No way, sweetie. That's one problem you have to deal with on your own." Trisha laughed and linked her arms with Kevin, leading him in the opposite direction of the figure, who was rushing toward Lizzie.

Chapter 7

Lizzie frowned as she watched her two best friends walk away, leaving her to deal with the approaching figure.

"Eliza! Eliza, I've been trying to reach you all day." The man shouted as he got closer, and Lizzie sighed even heavier. There was no getting out of it; she was going to have to talk to her cousin Freddie.

"I've been here all day, Freddie, and my phone's been on. I don't understand why you couldn't get ahold of me. What's the big emergency?"

"I wanted to come out and inspect the work that's being done on the old house." He paused for a moment, trying to catch his breath as he reached her side and then looked at her inquiringly, "Did you find anything?"

"You ask me that every time you come here, Freddie. I don't know what you think there is to find, or why you think you need to inspect what I'm doing. You always seem to forget Azalea Plantation is rightfully mine."

Lizzie regularly agitated her cousin by reminding him about the ownership of the plantation. It always led to an argument that she didn't feel was worth getting into. Her ancestor, Elizabeth, had stipulated in her will that Azalea Plantation was to always go to the female heir and not the oldest male, as was tradition. This was because Elizabeth had escaped an abusive husband with her children to her family's plantation. She was the only living relative her grandparents had, so the house went to her, along with the hundreds of acres set aside for cattle and horses and farming. A young woman with children in tow, she had done her best, selling some of the land to get by. As she had struggled, Elizabeth had vowed that she would never have one of her descendants go through the struggles that she did just because she was a woman. And each generation after that had honored Elizabeth's wishes, always leaving the plantation and property for the oldest female heir.

Freddie ignored her little dig. He was more curious about whether she had discovered anything from her ancestors while she had been renovating.

"You know exactly what I'm talking about. Did you find any clue where Elizabeth hid her treasure?"

"Oh, Freddie. When are you going to realize there is no treasure? If Elizabeth had had money with her when she came to the homestead, there would be none left after getting herself and her family established. There were cattle to be fed, and bills to be paid, and crops to be planted. There was never any extra money. It's just an old wives' tale."

Freddie shook his head as she spoke, disagreeing with the old argument they had every time they got together. Freddie was determined that because he was a male heir, he should get at least part of the treasure, even if he couldn't have the land or the homestead.

"I disagree. Everyone knows Elizabeth stole that money from the robbers when she made her escape. And she hid it somewhere on this property. Eventually, we're going to find it."

"We're?"

Freddie ignored her question and started toward Lizzie's new home, determined to see for himself what she had discovered. He walked up the front steps like he owned the place to open the door, without waiting for Lizzie to welcome him in. It was just the way Freddie was, and Lizzie didn't bother trying to argue with him.

But instead of the door opening easily as it had been, it seemed stuck, and Freddie reached out with both hands to tug. It was as if somebody was holding the door shut from the inside and then suddenly let go. The door flew open, and Freddie landed on his backside. Lizzie stifled a giggle, not wanting to embarrass her cousin any more than he was already.

"Who's inside that house trying to play tricks on me? I bet Trisha hurried around back just to aggravate me."

"I don't think so, Freddie. Look for yourself; there's Trisha and Kevin heading over toward the greenhouse. There was no way she could've held that door. I think it was just you."

"Nonsense, there was somebody holding that door. I don't know what you're playing at, Eliza."

"Freddie, you have so many problems when you're out here at the plantation. Why do you even bother coming around? You're not happy when you're here."

"I'm not happy because it should be mine," he muttered under his breath as he got to his feet.

Lizzie shrugged and ignored his mutterings. She'd heard it often enough as they were growing up together. Instead, she walked around him and went into the house. But when Freddie followed her, the door slammed shut, and Lizzie spun around in surprise. She hadn't even pushed on the door. She quickly hurried to open the door before Freddie could start ranting and raving about something else.

Once Freddie was in the main hallway, he looked around and couldn't help but be impressed with the renovation work that was being done.

"You sure lucked out. I still don't understand how this house was in such pristine condition for its age. I think you should rent it out rather than live here. You were perfectly okay in the upstairs suite over the main plantation. Think of the income you could get from this place."

"Freddie, let's not go there again. Frankly, it's none of your business. Come on, let's go to the kitchen. I'm sure Nora is still here, and she's going to want to show you all her hard work."

Lizzie grabbed her cousin's elbow and steered him toward the hallway that would lead to the kitchen, rather than letting him go up the stairs to the mezzanine, which is where he was trying to go. But at the mention of Nora, Freddie cheered up. As irritating as her cousin was, Nora always had a soft spot for him, making sure he never left after visiting without a hamper full of freshly cooked food and baked goods. It wasn't as though Freddie was indigent or needed her donations. Nora just felt he needed some home cooking. He had a large inheritance from his father's side of the family that he never offered to share with Lizzie, even though he expected her to share hers.

Freddie lived the life of luxury, and sometimes Lizzie wondered how much of his inheritance he had already spent. Had he been born in a different era, Lizzie could've accurately named him a dandy.

"Freddie, it's nice to see you." Giving the man a wide smile, Nora welcomed him into the kitchen. Freddie gave her a lukewarm smile and then looked around him, frowning at the kitchen's decor.

"Why didn't you modernize this room? Honestly, Eliza, why would you want to go back in time rather than forward? This looks like something out of another era. For crying out loud, there's a wood stove in here."

"Why spoil the ambiance of this beautiful old home with modern appliances? Lizzie had the right idea, and I think the results are wonderful," Nora surprised Lizzie with her answer, considering she had fought tooth and nail over Lizzie's idea of a retro-looking kitchen rather than a modern, efficient style.

Freddie wandered around the kitchen, looking into cupboards and opening the doors to the fridge and the oven. Lizzie ignored him, knowing he was going to have something detrimental to say about what he found, and turned her attention to Nora. But Nora wasn't paying attention to Lizzie or Freddie. Her gaze was fixed on something behind Lizzie.

"Nora?" Lizzie tried to get her attention, but the older woman just waved her hand and pointed. Lizzie turned quickly and saw the fluttering of a dark shadow walked past the kitchen door. A moment later, she turned back to Freddie and saw the hazy outline of the woman dressed in a long black dress with a white apron and white cap on her head. The woman looked up at Lizzie and Nora and winked, then she reached up and opened the cupboard door above the stove. When Freddie stood up from his inspection, he whacked his head on the door and spun around to see what had happened. But there was no one to see, and Lizzie and Nora were too far away for them to have done it.

"I don't know how you can stay in this house, Eliza. It's too creepy." Lizzie bit her lip to keep from laughing as the shadowy figure pushed a pile of hand towels behind Freddie's back, making them drop all over his feet. Whatever the ghost was up to, it had the effect she wanted. And Lizzie watched as Freddie hurriedly made his excuses and turned to leave through the kitchen door onto the terrace.

But he stopped full force when he saw all the equipment from the filming lying around where the crew had left it.

"You're even filming your own home? I don't know how you can have strangers walking around here all the time. Wasn't a murder at your retirement party enough to teach you to keep your private life away from prying eyes?"

Lizzie didn't react. The ghostly figure moved forward at a fast pace, and Lizzie was sure Freddie was going to get a push down that last step. But Nora stepped in between the two, causing the figure to halt. Nora gave a gentle shake of her head, and the ghost disappeared. Then Nora went forward to talk to

Freddie and, with a wave to Lizzie, guided Freddie back to the main house with the promise of lunch.

Lizzie stepped back into the kitchen and looked around. This was not the same specter that she had seen on other occasions, the specter of her ancestor Elizabeth, but she liked the recent addition's style.

"Thank you."

Still grinning at the bemused look on Freddie's face, Lizzie decided there was room in her new home for more than one ghost—especially if they taunted Freddie.

Chapter 8

The film crew quickly took advantage of Lizzie's offer for a light meal and to wander the gardens. They were being given a half day free of care and worries, and since Camille had left, little aggravation.

Emma watched as the girl with the bright pink hair loaded her plate and walked over to a bench to sit and enjoy her meal. After she had her fill of the delicious food, Emma wandered over to sit next to her. She gave the younger girl a friendly smile to put her at ease.

"So, Kelly, how do you like working on this film crew? And how did you land the job at this young age? How old are you?" With the unabashed nosiness of youth, Emma poured out her questions, but Kelly didn't seem offended by them, and she filled Emma in on a few of her details, but Emma couldn't help noticing she omitted telling how old she actually was.

"I like the work—a lot. And mostly everybody's pretty easy to work with. They all have their quirks and their personality dysfunctions, but I do my work and just stay away from everybody else. It's pretty easy to get pulled into the arguments with Camille." She took another bite of one of the chef's delicious brownies. "It was dumb luck that I ended up working for Camille. I was in between jobs, so to speak, and she just kinda found me, offered me a job as a gofer, and the pay was pretty good. Of course, when you're not working, any pay is good, isn't it?"

The two girls shared a laugh, and Emma paused for a moment, thinking how best to word her next question.

"Okay, I'm just going to say it—what's with Camille? I've never come across such a nasty woman in my life. It's like she goes out of her way to poke at people and push their buttons."

Kelly was silent for a moment, and then she slowly nodded. "You described it perfectly. Camille rules by sheer force and fear. It's almost as if she has something she's holding over everybody's head, and they bow to her wishes and commands for fear of her revealing what she knows."

Emma hesitated and then decided not to ask the obvious question. If Kelly wanted to talk about her troubles, she would, but Emma would not push her. She honestly felt the girl needed a friend, and being nosy would not win that friendship. Emma's mind was already making plans on how to find Kelly a different job in better circumstances. But she had to know more about the girl, and when Kelly was ready, she would tell her.

"How do you like working for Trisha and Kevin? They seem like they're really on the ball and easy to work for. What's it like having a place to stay out here at Azalea Plantation? I bet you can't wait for the end of the day when you can come back here and relax."

"Well, Trisha and Kevin grew up with Lizzie. So, they're all pretty thick. My mom went to college with Lizzie and Trisha and one other woman, and they were inseparable, so between all of them, they arranged for my internship, and Lizzie graciously offered me a place to stay. The timing was perfect. My mom had just gotten remarried, and I was kind of at a loss, not knowing what direction I was going in. The girl I was living with was also getting married, and I was feeling like a third wheel everywhere I turned. I had a degree in graphic design, and this seemed like a great extension to work with Kevin and Trisha. Who knows what will happen later, but for now it's pretty cool."

Kelly gave a nod of understanding, and Emma had a feeling she knew what it was like to be in the way of other people's lives. Not that Emma was in the way, but sometimes she couldn't help feeling that way. She had a sneaky suspicion that Kelly's sense of understanding came from more than casual knowledge.

"Staying here at Azalea Plantation is fantastic. There's a lot of family history here that Lizzie has been more than willing to share with me. Did you know there's a ghost that lives here? One of her ancestors who supposedly stole a train robber's heist, made her way back to the plantation, and started her own life here. Her home life was terrible, abusive from what they say." She paused when Kelly drew her breath in sharply but didn't push her new friend. "They never found the money, so everybody that comes here secretly is looking for it. Lizzie turns a blind eye to the searching, knowing full well they're never going to find anything. From what Trish told me, her and Kevin and Lizzie spent a lot of time in their youth searching every inch of the plantation trying to find that missing money."

The two girls shared a laugh at the image of a younger trio searching the plantation.

"That money is probably long gone," said Kelly as she wiped her mouth with a napkin.

"You got that right. I'd sure spend it in a heartbeat. Hey, if you're done eating, why don't we take a walk around? I'll show you the greenhouses and, on the way back, you can check out my cabin."

"I don't want to go too far and end up not having a ride back to town."

"That's not a problem. I've got my car here—I can always drive you back. You may as well spend the day and enjoy yourself. Heck, it's worth staying just to have one of the chef's incredible dinners. Nora dabbles in the kitchen, but it's the chef who makes the magic."

Kelly seemed relieved to have something to do that didn't involve being around the others, and she smiled in agreement. Gathering their plates and trash, Emma walked over to a nearby garbage can that was camouflaged by being set into a rock cropping. She knew that there was staff who came around and emptied the garbage cans that were scattered around the property once or twice a day. One of the big draws for the guests staying at Azalea Plantation was being able to wander the gardens. The research greenhouses attracted a lot of visitors too and there was even a gift shop off of the kitchen garden where Josh Bedingfield, the greenhouse and research manager, allowed some of their extra products to be sold.

"And if you want, after we eat, Lizzie has canoes over on the side of the house that we could take out into the pond. Nora will give us a head of lettuce and we can feed the swans. They love it."

Kelly gave a sigh of satisfaction, pleased with Emma's suggestions. "Thanks for including me. This sounds like a perfect day, to be honest."

As Emma and Kelly wandered the grounds, Emma couldn't help noticing the young girl became less nervous and opened up more about herself. She gave little specifics, but Emma gathered she was on her own with no family around her. She was living in a halfway house in downtown where the rent was cheap, and the landlady was pleasant and looked out for her. From what Kelly said, it seemed like she jumped from job to job as they were offered or as she moved around. Emma had a distinct feeling she was running from something but didn't want to ask too many personal questions.

They finished wandering through the research greenhouses, where Kelly had been fascinated by the work that Josh was doing. She asked intelligent questions, which earned her the privilege of Josh spending some time with her. He rarely mingled with the guests, preferring his own company and his research.

As they wandered the gardens, Emma noticed several others from the crew were still around as well. It seemed nobody wanted to go back to town. They rounded a corner on the path, and she pointed out a small building with window boxes overflowing, and a welcoming wraparound wood porch.

"There's my cabin. I've got some soda in there, and we can sit on the porch for a minute." Emma suggested as she waved a hand in greeting to Ophelia, who was walking toward the kitchen garden. The shy woman returned her wave and then scurried away like a little mouse.

"And you can dish about all those people you're working with. They seem so different from each other," Emma added.

"Boy, you got that right. A soda sounds perfect right now. Lead the way."

With a laugh, Emma led the way down the side path that took them to the cottage she was staying in. These used to be old servants' quarters for families that lived on the plantation. They'd been renovated over the years and were rented out along with the rooms in the mansion for guests who came for vacations or just a quick getaway. Lizzie had deliberately given Emma the last cottage on the row so that she would have more privacy. It was set away a bit more from the other guest cottages and had a separate pathway. She was perfectly safe here but also had a sense of it being her own place without feeling part of the day-to-day activities around the plantation. It was simply decorated, and old furniture dotted the inside. On the porch, which is where Emma spent her free time watching the wildlife and the patrons of the plantation, were a series of overstuffed wicker chairs that invited you to sit and relax. At the far end of the porch was an old-fashioned wicker swing that hung from the rafters, big enough for three people to sit in.

"This is perfect." Kelly looked around and couldn't hide the envy in her voice.

"Isn't it? I can't believe my luck at having this all to myself. I take all my meals at the main house, but there is a kitchenette if I want to make something for myself."

Emma watched Kelly look around, taking in the pictures on the wall and the scattered personal items across the living area.

"I guess I'm not the best housekeeper. Sorry for the mess."

"No, no problem at all. Did you take those pictures?"

"No, those were done by one of my mom's roommates. She supplied a lot of the pictures here for Lizzie when she redecorated."

"They're stunning. She has a good eye for the camera. I bet she would be great at directing."

"I don't know about that. I know she just opened her own gallery down south, and she does a lot of classes teaching novices how to use their cameras."

"It's nice to have a niche where you can create your own sense of well-being."

Emma couldn't help but hear the wistfulness in Kelly's voice and quickly changed the subject, so she didn't embarrass her new friend. Shoving a soda in her hand, Emma led the way back out onto the porch. They each sat in one of the overstuffed chairs, watching the occasional guest that walked down the path close by. As they sipped their soda's, both girls were silent. Their eyelids were getting droopy as they relaxed to the sound of the chirping mockingbirds while the gentle breeze played with their hair. It was when Emma almost dropped her soda bottle, drifting into a relaxed stupor, that she jumped to her feet.

"I don't know about you, but if I sit here any longer, I'm going to be sound asleep." She glanced at her watch. "We've got about forty-five minutes before dinner. Why don't we take the boat out on the pond now, instead of later?"

"It's a great idea. It'll help us build up an appetite, right?"

"No problems there. The food here is so good it's hard not to have an appetite. Come on, you'll love these boats. Lizzie definitely has a sense of humor."

Kelly looked at Emma, wondering what she meant, but didn't say a word. Getting to her feet, she followed Emma's quick pace down the side path. In no time, the path ended as they emerged from the overhanging trees. There was a short dock and boathouse close by. Tied to the dock were different types of kayaks and, of all things, paddle boats in the shape of swans.

Emma led the way down the dock and turned to wave her hand at the array of kayaks.

"You can take your pick. There are glass bottom kayaks, old-fashioned kayaks, and these ridiculous swan paddle boats. She bought those on a lark because of the swans that have made their home here. The guests love them, especially the kids."

"Well then, I guess I'm a kid at heart, because I'd love to try one out."

Emma smiled and grabbed a rope to untie one of the swan paddle boats from the pilings. "I had a feeling you would."

Laughing, the two girls got in the boat and adjusted the seat so that they could easily reach the pedals. Then, giggling and laughing, they slowly backed away from the dock and circled the pond.

The pond was quite large, and there were little canals that joined the pond to the river system that ran along the property line of the plantation. In the distance, they could see two pairs of swans gliding gracefully.

"Look, Kelly, there's the swans," Emma pointed in the birds' direction, and Kelly grinned at the graceful picture they made. Then both girls noticed something odd: the birds would glide along, and then suddenly, their wings would flap, and they would move away from something, only to glide along and come back to it. Whatever it was, it had their curiosity, but they were also clearly afraid of it.

"I wonder what's going on out there. There's never anything in the water that would scare them. Lizzie makes sure the wildlife patrol comes out and checks for gators and anything that might want to make a meal out of them."

"Do you mean alligators? Is it safe to be out here?"

"It's perfectly safe. Even though the pond is fed by the river, it's unusual to find a gator out here. And if they do, they just take it deeper into its natural habitat. As long as the guests don't feed him, he really has no interest here. There's plenty of wild fish and game along the riverbanks, away from the pond."

As Emma spoke, she guided the boat toward the swans. Together the two girls pedaled quickly, and in no time, they were coming up to the area the swans were trying to avoid.

"What is that in the water?" Kelly asked, squinting against the setting sun.

Emma didn't answer. Instead, she precariously stood up, trying to get a better look. And then wished she hadn't. She gave a startled scream and plopped back down in her seat. Kelly looked at Emma and then back to the area the swans were avoiding, and she also stood up in the boat, rocking it dangerously.

"Oh my God!"

"You see it too? We better get help."

"I don't think there's any help for her."

Both girls looked back, shivering at the sight of Camille floating in the water, her curly hair bobbing around her head, her eyes wide open, but seeing nothing.

Chapter 9

Lizzie and Kevin were walking from the front porch of her house to head down the winding path toward the main house when they heard a female scream from the pond.

"That was Emma, and Kelly!"

Lizzie pointed toward the two girls. They were easy to spot; Kelly's bright pink hair was a sharp contrast to the white of the swan paddle boat. Emma was waving her hands frantically to get their attention.

"They're in some kind of trouble," Kevin shouted as he started running in the dock's direction, Lizzie close on his heels. As Lizzie followed, she turned around and spotted Josh, her greenhouse manager, and several of his staff members walking in the opposite direction toward the main house. She called out his name and motioned to the pond, and he immediately picked up the pace, ordering the others to follow. They all converged at the dock about the same time, and Lizzie and Kevin immediately jumped in the small, motorized boat that was also tied up on the dock and headed toward the two girls. Just as they were pulling away from the dock, Josh jumped in the boat with them, and in no time, they were close to the girls and cut their engine.

"She's dead, oh my God, she's dead. She's dead!"

Kelly's voice screeched as she pointed in Camille's direction. Josh immediately pulled their boat closer and held onto it so both boats were side by side, while Lizzie and Kevin looked to Emma for an explanation.

"About four yards ahead is where she's at. We were trying to figure out what the swans were so afraid of, and we found the body. Camille is floating in the water, and she's obviously gone."

Without a word, Kevin looked at his phone and dialed 911, asking for a certain detective he knew well. He gave a brief explanation and then turned to Josh and Lizzie.

"Josh, take the girls back to the dock. The detective will be here as quickly as possible. I'll stay here with the body."

"I'll stay with you. Josh, can you climb in with the girls to help them paddle back? We might need this boat to transport Camille back to dry land."

Lizzie would not leave Kevin by himself out in the pond with a dead body. Nobody should be left with that. She trusted Josh to take charge. Once he got the girls back, she knew he would inform the rest of the staff and Trisha about what had happened. By the time Lizzie and Kevin returned to land, everyone on the plantation would know about their gruesome find, she was sure. But what had happened?

"Are you okay if we get closer to the body?" They were silent as they watched Josh paddle the girls back toward the dock, but now Kevin wanted to secure the body if he could, even if it just meant staying next to it. He didn't know if there were currents in the pond other than what the main center fountain put out, and he didn't want to chance the body moving from the location they had found it in before the police got there.

"Yes, I'm fine. It's not as though I haven't seen a dead body before. Although I wish I didn't have to see this one in my pond." She looked toward the main entrance of the plantation, where she could hear the distant sounds of police sirens approaching. "It won't be long before they're here. As ghoulish as it sounds, I want to look at the body."

Kevin looked like he was going to say something, but he shook his head and grabbed one oar lying in the boat's bottom. He gently guided the boat to where Camille's body lay floating on the surface. The swans were swimming at a distance, but every once in a while, they would glide closer, as if their curiosity couldn't keep them away. When they reached the body, Lizzie looked down at the young woman, her short dark curls forming a halo around her head, the lightweight linen shirt floating around her upper body.

"What's that around her neck?"

"Lizzie, the very last thing the detective said was for you to stay out of it. Don't start asking questions. Let the police handle it."

"As if." Lizzie muttered under her breath and leaned forward over the edge of the boat to get a closer look. Kevin sighed heavily and steadied the boat so she wouldn't flip them over. But he also got a good look at what she was talking about, and he raised his eyebrows in surprise.

"I think it's an electric cord. There have been enough of them floating around on the terrace from all the equipment. Do you think she had it with her as she was leaving, or did her killer use it to strangle her?" Lizzie looked like she was going to reach out even farther, and Kevin used the oar to turn the boat slightly, so the body was further from her reach. She glanced at him, ready to ask what he was doing.

"I can't stop you from looking, but we won't tamper with the evidence before the police even get here."

"All right. You're right, of course. But I don't even know why she's here. We saw her grab the keys from one of her assistants and leave. That had to have been a couple of hours ago."

"Well, she came back."

"Yes, but was it of her own free will? Or did she come back to meet her killer?"

Lizzie and Kevin stared at each other, both knowing full well they were going to be asking a lot more questions. Lizzie would not let the detective slow her down, and if there was a killer on her property, she wanted to know about it.

Was it a stranger who had watched the filming, or was it one of the crew members?

Kevin was asking himself the same questions, as well as wondering if there was still danger around them.

THE POLICE ARRIVED quickly, and within an hour; they had dragged the body from the pond and had laid it out in a body bag on dry land. A detective was taking meticulous notes on what he saw, while two other officers were questioning everyone on the property. The detective had distinctly told the officers not to question the crew, Lizzie, Kevin, Trisha, and Emma. He wanted to do that himself. They were to concentrate on the plantation guests and those onlookers for the garden show filming. Finishing his notes, he flipped the cover to his tablet, closing the electronic device and turned to stare at Lizzie and Kevin.

"Why is it you two are in the middle of another murder? And how does it happen that this is the second murder out here on your property, Lizzie Higgins?"

"Well, it's not as though I invited them. Do you think I want this type of notoriety associated with the plantation?" Libby sputtered as she shoved her hands on her hips and stared, astonished at the detective's questions.

Kevin hid his smile. He knew full well his friend was trying to get a rile out of Lizzie, and he was succeeding. He caught the glance of the detective and gave a slight shake of his head. This wasn't the time to get under Lizzie's skin. Whether the detective accepted it, he was going to need Lizzie's help to solve this murder. Just like she had helped him before.

Chapter 10

Lizzie knew full well the detective wanted to talk to her again, but as soon as she had the chance, she slipped away. She could only take so much of his questions, and she had a few of her own. Trisha watched her walk away and quickly ran after her, leaving Kevin to handle the detective questioning the film crew.

"Well, what do you think? Was she definitely murdered? Ugh, it's so ghastly," Trisha shuddered as she spoke.

"I agree. Let's hope Emma and Kelly won't suffer any nightmares because of their discovery. I can't imagine how they felt coming upon Camille. It had become a peaceful afternoon, and they were having a great time."

Lizzie paused for a moment and glanced over to where Emma and Kelly were standing, away from the rest of the crew. The shock of what they had found had made Kelly seem even younger than Lizzie had first thought, and she couldn't help but feel a touch of protectiveness toward her.

"It was definitely murder," Lizzie turned her attention back to Trisha, remembering what she had seen, "there was some kind of electric cord wrapped around her neck. That had to be the murder weapon."

"Well, there were certainly enough of those lying around on the terrace. But I thought Camille had left. She sure made a show of leaving. How did she end up in the pond?"

"I have no idea. Like you, I thought she'd left. I remember her taking the keys from Ophelia and heading toward the van. But I can't honestly say I remember her driving away."

"Do you think she got intercepted by someone?"

"Seems to be the only thing that would make sense. It would have to be somebody she knew, or at least was familiar with, to make her go with them." Lizzie replied thoughtfully.

Trisha gave a short bark of laughter. "I disagree with that. That woman had such an ego, all that would take was a fan to call out a question, and she would go right over to them. If you think about it, she'd be an easy target."

"You're probably right. She was certainly full of herself. And I can't say that I saw any overly friendly gestures toward her from her crew. Whenever they weren't working with her, everyone was doing their best to stay away."

"I don't know about you, sweetie, but I've got a lot of questions. I didn't particularly like the woman, but she was working for me, and I feel sort of responsible."

Lizzie gave an absent nod, her attention focused on somebody walking across the lawn toward her house. It took her a moment to recognize the figure. When she did, she turned to Trisha.

"I think we've got more trouble. Isn't that Kate Baxter heading toward my house? If she's here sniffing around, who knows what kind of article she'll write for the paper? I'm sure it won't be favorable."

"Oh crap. You're right, that is Kate. Come on, we need to run interception and fast. The best thing we can do is give her a no comment and try to get her away from the property."

Before Lizzie could answer, her phone buzzed, and she looked down to see there was a text message coming from Josh. She skimmed through it and groaned.

"We might be too late. Josh just messaged me and said Kate had been snooping around the greenhouse. Who knows how long she's been here or what she's heard or seen?"

"There's only one way to find out. Let me apply some of my southern charm and find out what she's up to." Trisha gave an exaggerated batting of her eyes and motioned for Lizzie to follow her as she sped off toward the house.

When they were close enough to the woman with the dark hair, Trisha yelled out a friendly greeting.

"Kate Baxter, fancy seeing you here. It's such a beautiful day. I hope you're enjoying yourself."

"When you said you would apply the charm, you weren't kidding. I think you're pouring it on too heavy. Tone it down a bit, Trisha, or she'll know you're up to something," hissed Lizzie, trying to keep laughter from bubbling to the surface.

"Catch them with honey, not vinegar. Always remember that, Lizzie." Trisha grinned back at her best friend and then turned a megawatt smile toward Kate Boxer.

The pretty woman was younger than Trisha and Lizzie and was dressed smartly in business attire. She had a tablet in her hands that she opened up, ready to take comments from the two coming toward her. She had a working relationship with Trisha, but she wasn't overly friendly toward Lizzie. Trisha had pointed out that Kate had designs on Kevin and considered Lizzie an obstacle in reaching her objective. And Kate thrived on obstacles. When the women got close enough to Kate, Trisha air kissed the young woman and asked how she was doing.

"Well, I came out to see a film crew and stumbled on one of the best stories I've had in a long time. Can I get quotes from you two on what's going on out here?"

Kate wouldn't be mollified. She went right for the jugular, trying to figure out what was going on. She had a deadline to meet and if she could get the scoop before any other reporter, that just made her career go up another notch.

"Hello, Kate," Lizzie said, stretching out her hand to be shaken, not allowing the young woman to ignore her.

"Hi, Lizzie. Had quite an active morning out here, haven't you?"

Trisha was all ready to go into protection mode and try to keep Kate from finding out any information, but Lizzie stopped her, deciding to turn the tables on the reporter.

"It's shocking, really. We'd finished some setups for filming and then closed down for the day. Everybody was eager to get the lay of the land and explore the gardens. You know how that feels, don't you, Kate?"

Kate gave Lizzie a sharp look and then slowly smiled when she understood Lizzie's reference to having wandered around rather than making her presence known.

"It's hard not to wander these gardens. And you know as well as I do the projects that Josh Bedingfield is working on makes your greenhouses newsworthy. I was just wandering around trying to find out if any new information was available on his latest gardening triumph." She paused for dramatic effect and then continued, "Who knew while trying to find out about some hybrid roses, I would stumble on another murder out here at Azalea Plantation. What do you say, Lizzie? Is the plantation cursed?"

Lizzie smiled broadly, entertained by the young woman's train of thought. "Last time you were here, you accused me of having a ghost hiding treasures. Now you're telling me my plantation is cursed? You have quite the imagination, Kate. I'll tell you what. I'll make sure you're the first reporter notified when the rose Josh is perfecting is ready. You can have an exclusive."

"And in return?"

"Smart girl. Yes, I want something in return. I want you to share anything you find out about this murder with me before you print it, please."

"And will you reciprocate?"

All Lizzie did was smile, letting the woman interpret it how she wanted. Trisha had watched the interaction between the two and was pleased to see some of the Lizzie she had known in college come through. She'd been a professor for so long that she had fallen into the political practice of politeness. She was quickly learning it was a give and take world outside of academia. And the old Lizzie could hold her own under any circumstances. The Lizzie in front of her had only gotten better with age.

"You know, I'm sure Nora has stocked Lizzie's kitchen with plenty of soda and her homemade lemonade. Why don't we go up on the porch, get comfortable, and share our gossip? What do you say, girls?" Trisha grabbed the elbow of each of the other two and nodded toward the welcoming front porch. Lizzie and Kate exchanged a look and nodded, accepting that an agreement had just been formed.

Chapter 11

Detective Richard Mendoza stared at his friend, waiting for an explanation of where Lizzie had disappeared to. He still had questions for her. Kevin hemmed and hawed, not wanting to admit Lizzie had given them both the slip. The two men were walking away from the pier; by now the body had been removed, and Richard was ready to question the suspects all over again. The morning sun was heating the afternoon air, and a slight breeze was making the water on the pond ripple.

Things had calmed down considerably since the detectives' arrival a few hours earlier. Guests from the plantation had been redirected to the gardens and away from the crime scene. Nora Meadows was handling the daily deliveries with her usual efficiency, keeping the drivers from asking nosy questions about the police and the crime scene tape around the pond, while making sure the staff were kept too busy to gossip. There would be plenty of time for that later.

The chef, Thomas Ranger, had set up a small coffee station for the police to help themselves and then he had directed his kitchen staff to their chores, taking it upon himself to refill the coffee pots as needed.

"I don't know whether to be frustrated that she is giving me the slip or relieved. Last time she got in my way—"

"She may have been in the way, but you have to admit she helped solve who killed the new professor."

"You can wipe that smirk off your face, Kevin. This isn't some TV show where the cutesy little librarian solves the crimes. This is real life, and someone has been murdered. It's my job to find out who and why. Not you, not your friends. Are we clear on that?"

"Trust me, Richard, that's a job you can have. I want nothing to do with it. But I have a feeling I'm going to get sucked into it again. You'd better look over toward Lizzie's house."

The detective followed Kevin's line of sight and groaned out loud. "Oh, that can't be good."

The two men watched Lizzie, Kate, and Trisha talking before they turned and headed toward Lizzie's house. Secretly, Kevin agreed this would not be good. Kate didn't get along very well with Lizzie, and for them to be joining forces, even briefly, spelled trouble.

Before either of them could continue the conversation, another officer yelled for the detective and waved his arms, pointing toward the vehicles that had been driven in by the film crew. Kevin watched Richard's eyes narrow, and his brow wrinkled as he watched the figure of a man moving slowly toward the first van in line.

Richard pushed a button on his lapel and spoke into his radio. "Stop the man before he gets in the van. It's still considered part of the crime scene, and nobody leaves here until I talk to them again." Richard watched closely as his officer stepped forward and spoke to the younger man who was getting ready to open the door to the van. The man seemed to argue for a moment with the officer and then threw up his arms in frustration, turned around, and walked back toward the area where they had been filming.

"Looks like I need to smooth some feathers here. I'll deal with Lizzie later." Richard said. "You may as well come with me. I think the film crew falls under the category of subcontractor for your company, am I right?"

Kevin gave a nod, quickly assessing that Richard was going to use him as a buffer to keep things friendly as he spoke to the suspects. He was used to Richard's methods; they'd been friends for a long time, and this was a tactic he'd used not only as a police officer but in his day-to-day life. His motto was to keep people comfortable and then pounce when they weren't expecting it. It worked for him.

As Richard and Kevin started toward the patio where they had been filming, Richard quickly gave instructions to his officers to round up all the suspects. Then he grinned over at Kevin. "The first round was individual questions. Now let's see what happens when they're asked questions as a group. Are they going to support each other or turn on each other? What are the odds? Kevin, you want to put money on the chance they'll turn on each other?"

Kevin grinned at his friend. Richard would bet on just about anything, not for hard-core money, but for the bragging rights of being correct more times than not. But this time, Kevin thought Richard might be wrong. The group that Camille had assembled all seemed to protect each other. At first, it was just protecting each other from Camille, but Kevin wondered if that would continue when the finger started pointing at individual suspects.

Like a powerful magnet pulling pieces of metal toward it, the film crew made its way to the back patio of Lizzie's renovated home. They came from different directions, and Kevin couldn't help noticing they came individually except for Kelly Sky. Emma accompanied her, talking as they walked. Kevin watched the two of them walk slowly, hesitantly, across the lawn. He knew it was inevitable the two of them would be tied together because they were the ones who discovered the body, and that tragic experience was a bond that would never be broken. But as he watched Emma put her arm protectively around Kelly's shoulder, he had a feeling there was a friendship that was going to be deeper.

Before he could say a word to Richard, the figure of a small man appeared at the corner of the house. Lizzie's cousin Freddy, swinging his head from side to side, stepped out from behind the large azalea bush that covered most of the back corner of the house. After another look around, assuring himself he wasn't being watched, Freddy shut the door behind him. Keven frowned. He thought the man had left. If he was still here, that could only mean trouble.

Chapter 12

Emma paused what she was saying to Kelly and looked around her. She felt like she was being watched, but as she looked, she could see nobody staring at her. Looking farther away from her immediate area, she caught sight of Kevin and the detective. She gave a wave to acknowledge she had seen them. She and Kelly had been told by one of the other officers to meet over at the terrace by the old fireplace, and that was where they were heading.

They were in no hurry to get there, and Emma could feel the heat radiating from her new friend. It was more than just the reaction of finding Camille's body. There was something else bothering Kelly, but Emma would not push her for answers. Kelly looked up from the ground to see what Emma was waving at and visibly cringed when she saw the detective.

"Why do you think he wants to talk to us again?" Kelly took a deep breath as if to steady herself. "There's nothing more I can help them with about Camille."

"I'm sure he has plenty of questions. The last time there was a murder here, I found him to be very thorough and considerate. He does his job, Kelly, but you have nothing to hide, and he is not going to spend much time with you."

Kelly looked at her friend, her mouth hanging open in surprise. "Did you say the last time they found a murder on the plantation? How awful!"

"Yes, it happened at Lizzie's retirement party. Lizzie quickly jumped into the middle of the investigation, and I don't think the detective was all that happy about it. But she's smart, and she could find out things he couldn't. In the end, they worked together and solved it. But I don't think either of them ever expected to have to be going through it again."

"Goodness, you'd think one murder is more than enough in a lifetime." Kelly gave a mock shudder and changed the topic of the conversation by asking about Emma's involvement in the production company. Emma answered her question, but she couldn't help but note that Kelly never made a comment about whether she had something to hide, and her curiosity rose.

She answered Kelly's question, and then as casually as she could, asked one of her own. "How did you get involved with Camille?"

Kelly hesitated, clearly torn about whether she wanted to answer Emma's question or not. Finally, she gave a drawn-out sigh, as if a huge decision had been made, and she turned to Emma with a grimace.

"It started out as a positive life change. I was desperate for work, and Camille offered me a job. And that would've been great except for Camille's obsession with being a collector."

"I'm sorry, a collector?"

"Yes, a collector, a collector of people, a collector of secrets, and a collector of opportunities to use something against somebody."

"She sounds horrid. Why did you stay working with her?"

Kelly looked Emma directly in Emma's eyes, and Emma could see the young girl had troubles beyond her years.

"I told you I was desperate. You may as will hear it from me because it's going to come out, eventually. She knew I was desperate for a job because I'm a runaway. I was tired of being shipped off from foster parent to foster parent, each one less interested in me as I grew older. I finally decided if they weren't going to be interested in me, I had to fight for myself, and I took off. That was a year ago. I was really down on my luck when I stumbled across Camille on a shoot. I don't know how she zoned in on me, but before I knew it, she had given me a job and advanced me some cash to tide me over. She wanted me to live with her, but I refused. I'd rather live on the streets than be in debt to anybody."

"I'm so sorry, Kelly."

"It was working out really well. I was putting some money aside, and I really thought I was going to be able to go to school next year. But then Camille started using my secrets against me. Before long, I was doing things for her I never would've on my own." Kelly saw the look on Emma's face and quickly added, "I did nothing illegal, but I helped her collect secrets. I spied on people for her. It's not something I'm proud of, and to be honest, her death means I'm free of it."

Emma heard the relief in Kelly's voice as she realized she would not have to do Camille's dirty work any longer. The younger girl looked at Emma and smiled wistfully. "Her death is giving me freedom. But what do I do with it?"

Emma reached over and squeezed Kelly's hand. "You take things one step at a time. The first thing is to find Camille's killer. Maybe some of those secrets you helped her collect holds an answer."

"Maybe, but I will not turn on other people the way Camille did. The police are smart; they can find the answers for themselves. I will not become Camille."

Emma gave a tug on Kelly's hand, and started toward the fireplace where they were to meet the others. As they walked, Emma grinned at her new friend.

"Maybe there's another way to go about this. We need to talk to Lizzie. She'll know what to do."

"What do you think is going to happen to the production company and those of us working on it?"

"Well, I know Trisha and Kevin, and they don't like to leave things unfinished. Somehow, they'll work it out that you can continue working. We'll take things step-by-step, but first, let's get this interview over with the police, then we can concentrate on your more immediate needs."

"I suppose you're right. This definitely changes things."

"Don't worry, Kelly, I'll think of something. You're not gonna be left on the streets if I can help it."

"Don't worry about me. I'll find someplace. I'm actually glad I can't go back to Camille's. Even if I wasn't living with her, I was there so much I often spent the night on her couch."

Emma looked at Kelly with a grin, one her mother would recognize as a sign of trouble to come. She stared at Kelly until the younger girl could stand it no longer.

"What?"

"I have a couch in my cabin. If you could stay with Camille, then you can crash with me. And we don't even have to tell anyone."

"How are you going to keep that secret?"

"Easy. You're still going to be filming out here. Just tell the rest of the crew you have your own way to get here, and no one will be the wiser. It's a big place, and with the guests that come and go, no one from the main house will even notice you're staying with me."

The two girls looked back toward Emma's cabin and then back to each other and slowly Kelly returned Emma's grin.

"It might work," she whispered.

Chapter 13

Lizzie and Trisha had been the first to arrive on the back patio after receiving the message, via a text from Kevin, that Detective Mendoza wanted to speak to everyone a second time. After talking with Kate, they'd gone back inside to continue putting books on the shelves. It was something to pass the time as they waited for the next step in the investigation.

"Well, at least Kate's out of the way for the second round of interviews." Trisha said, as she peered over Lizzie's shoulder to read the text message.

"Yes, I'm sure the detective will appreciate her absence." She hesitated for a moment and then looked at Trisha, worry clear in her eyes. "Did I just make a deal with the devil agreeing to work with Kate?"

Trisha couldn't help but laugh at her question or the look on her face. "It's better to be working with her than against her. At least this way you know what she's up to."

"You're right, but I still feel uneasy."

"Well, let's put it this way, Lizzie; having Kate look into the background of Camille is going to raise less suspicion than if you and I do it. There are other avenues you and I can pursue. And whether he likes it, Detective Mendoza is giving us the perfect opportunity."

"He is, isn't he? Questioning everybody at once is bound to bring out information, and he's going to be so busy concentrating on what's being said he's not going to notice the interaction between people as he questions them."

The two women exchanged grins, and Lizzie looked across the lawn where she could see Kevin and the detective working their way toward the patio. For a moment, she hesitated. The detective had proven himself to be smarter than what she gave him credit for once before. She had a feeling there wasn't much that he was going to miss—she was just going to be faster than him. After all, she wasn't held by rules and regulations of law to the same degree as an investigating officer. She could just be nosy and ask questions.

"Looks like everybody got the message." Trisha said, as she pointed to small groups of people making their way across the lawn. A couple were coming from the greenhouse and gardens, others from the back kitchen entry to the plantation where the chef was sure to have fed them well. Oddly enough, nobody was coming from the direction of the pond. Everybody had been giving it a wide berth. Of course, having the police tape around the entry to the pier was a not-so-subtle reminder of what had taken place. Within five minutes, they were all seated around a large makeshift picnic table that had been set up for the crew. It had been put there to help hold their equipment, but now it had become an interrogation table, with the detective standing at the head of the table while the others sat in chairs looking up at him, squinting against the afternoon sun. The detective made sure he had made eye contact with each of the suspects before he cleared his throat and spoke.

"Thank you for being so prompt. I know I've spoken to each of you individually, but now I need to speak to you as a group. Maybe together you will remember something. Let's clarify that your cooperation in my interrogation is going to make it go smoother and faster so that you can get back to your lives as quickly as possible. I need you to realize you are not to leave town until the investigation is completed. I am assuming you will continue working here at the Azalea Plantation?" The detective's question was directed at Trisha and Kevin, who vigorously nodded in agreement. Not only did they have a production to get done, but they also understood that having everybody on-site for as much time as possible would better the chances of closing the case quickly. "Fine. Let's start with the simple question. What was Camille's mood like today? Did she seem normal, under stress, afraid of anything? Can you think of anything out of the ordinary?"

There was silence as each of the suspects thought about their day with Camille. As miserable as the woman was, Lizzie got the feeling that was normal for her, and after a few moments of silence, it was Tony who spoke first. "I don't know about the rest of you, but I saw nothing unusual about Camille's demeanor. She was the same miserable person she always was."

"Tony, that's not fair. She had a lot of pressure on her shoulders—" Tony cut off Ophelia's interruption with a large bark of laughter.

"Oh, knock it off, Ophelia. You know as well as I do what she was like, and today was no different. If she wasn't barking out orders, she was demeaning everybody here. Maybe I'm the only honest one here, but I'm not gonna miss being yelled at and demeaned by Camille."

The two of them stared at each other for a moment, and then Ophelia gave a slight nod of her head, conceding that Tony was right. Tony's outburst was like a small stone being let loose from the dam and the water poured out, or rather the complaints about Camille. The detective was busy writing what the suspects had to say, and he kept control of the situation, letting them let loose their pent-up emotions.

Lizzie thought he was so busy trying to make sure he got every word, he wasn't paying attention to the silent communications between Camille's staff, but she wasn't missing a thing. Lizzie had the distinct impression that each one of them was hiding something, but until she could talk to them or snoop around a bit more, it was going to be some time before she found out what they were hiding. They might verbalize their distaste for their boss, but they weren't letting their own secrets out. Not in front of the detective.

Kevin and Trisha exchanged a glance with Lizzie, and it was clear they had come to the same assessment. Lizzie listened for a while longer, but soon realized she was hearing the same complaints about Camille's unreasonable demands, nasty demeanor, and outright meanness. She was going to have to talk to the suspects on their own, and she looked from one to the other, wondering which was the weakest link, the one that would share their secret in order to clear their name. Before she could decide who to approach first, she stuffed her hands into her pockets and felt a piece of paper. She'd forgotten all about stuffing the note in her pocket earlier. She pulled it out and reread the message. This might be the way to get things out in the open. At least it would give the detective a new angle. She knew she had to give it to him and this seemed like the perfect time. Stepping forward from behind the detective, she placed a piece of paper on the table in front of him, tapping on it to draw his attention to the wording.

"What's this, Lizzie?"

"I don't know when it was given to Camille, but she opened it this morning while she was out here on the terrace. She crumpled it up and threw it away when she thought no one was looking. Harry and I went back later and retrieved it. I don't know if it has anything to do with her murder, but it is interesting, don't you think?"

The detective exchanged a look with Lizzie and gave a curt nod. She was right. This was an interesting piece of information. By now, everyone was staring at Lizzie and the detective, their eyes darting between the two standing at the head of the table and the piece of paper that sat on the table. Looking around at his suspects, the detective cleared his throat and read the note out loud.

"Now, would any of you like to tell me what this note is about?"

Chapter 14

The tone of detective Mendoza's voice allowed for no misunderstanding. The man wanted answers, and he would not budge until the group gave him what he was looking for. Lizzie lowered her eyes just enough that she wasn't looking at anybody directly but could still see them squirming as they waited for him to speak.

Kelly Sky was sitting next to Emma, nervously twisting her bright pink hair. She was one of the few not looking at the detective. Lizzie knew instinctively, from years of teaching, that Kelly was hiding something. She may answer the detective's questions, but they would be half-truths. Lizzie made a note to herself to talk to the young woman after the detective was done.

Ophelia was looking everywhere, nervously picking at the pages of the notebook she held. She seemed more nervous about a confrontation with the detective than should have been warranted. Lizzie also remembered how Camille had berated and put her down and wondered if this wasn't a normal reaction to being around somebody in control.

"I haven't got a clue what that note means. I just know it has nothing to do with me."

Everyone's eyes turned to the quiet man sitting at the edge of the group, not quite part of it. Lizzie frowned as she tried to remember who he was and what his position was within the company. Then she remembered somebody saying he was a groupie following Camille around like a puppy, and the group had laughed at the description. But he didn't look so much like a puppy dog right now. He looked a little fierce, as if he was trying to protect Camille's memory.

"Earl, if anybody would know what that note means, it would be you. You're always shadowing Camille, and she knew you were. I think there isn't much about our former boss that you don't know." Tiffany was the one who spoke, flipping her long dark hair over her shoulders, tilting her head upright as if daring the other man to challenge her words. Ophelia and Kelly both nodded in agreement with Tiffany's words, and Tony just smirked, watching to see how Earl would react with the spotlight on him.

"Earl Chambers. You're not on the roster of employees for Camille Shoots. So why are you here?" The detective turned his attention to Earl, who squirmed as if he regretted opening his mouth.

Before he answered, Tony let out a bark of laughter, and explained to the detective Earl's position, getting in a few jabs at the same time.

"Oh, Earl here doesn't work for Camille. He's just an adoring fan. He follows Camille around from job site to job site. And she wasn't above taking advantage of that. How many times did you fetch her coffee today, Earl?"

Earl pushed his chair back as he tried to get to his feet, but his moves were jerky, and he clumsily plopped back down on the chair. Tony grinned meanly when the older man shouted at Tony, who merely gave a shrug of his shoulders, as if amused at the defensive reaction from the older man.

"Why don't you tell us what your relationship with Camille was all about? Now is your chance to be understood." The detective leaned forward, looking directly at Earl, his voice soothing, but his eyes hardened.

"I knew Camille when she was nothing. She was working on the jobs just like you guys are. She was a smart woman, and she quickly worked her way up. Before anybody even realized what was going on, she had bought out the company and changed the name. I've heard her called a lot of things: ruthless, miserly, vicious and even evil. But Camille had a good side to her. One she only showed me. So, while it may have looked like I was groveling, and being her gofer, we had an understanding. A friendship that was special, one only we could understand."

As Earl spoke, his voice became firmer, and he sat straighter in his chair. But those around the table were not nodding in agreement, instead they were giving him pitying looks, and Lizzie had the distinct impression the man was slightly delusional. Ophelia confirmed her suspicion.

"Earl, how can you still be protective of her when she treated you like dirt? There was no special relationship. And Camille wasn't friends with anybody; she was a user. And she used you, just like she used the rest of us." Ophelia finished speaking and closed her lips firmly as if afraid anymore words would come out.

Lizzie exchanged a glance with Trisha, and they turned their attention to the others at the table. It was clear the rest of the crew agreed with Ophelia, and there was no pity sent in Earl's direction. Only the distinct disdain one would give an outcast.

"You're wrong, you know. And I know Camille knew stuff about each one of you, stuff she told me in confidence." Earl huffed, looking at each of them, trying to make himself feel important. But the others at the table acted as if they weren't bothered by his words. Perhaps they had heard it all before.

The detective showed interest in Earl's proclamation, but when he pushed the man for more details, Earl closed up and refused to answer any other questions. The detective then turned his attention to the others but got no more information from them than he had before. Everyone had thought Camille had left for the day, and no one knew, or would admit, any reason somebody would want to kill her.

"All right. We're getting nowhere here. I understand you are going to continue to work here on Azalea Plantation. I don't want you to leave the grounds other than to go back to your hotel room. There'll be more questions later." Detective Mendoza stood up, pushing his chair back and looking disgustedly at the others sitting around him. Then he caught Kevin's attention and jerked his head toward the main plantation house. Without a word, Kevin also stood and followed the detective toward the main house.

There was a moment of silence, and then everybody turned to Lizzie as if waiting for directions from her. She looked at Trisha and nodded for her friend to do the speaking.

"The detective's right. As long as we have to be here, we may as well continue our job. I assume each of you knows how to do your job. We'll have to provide you with the direction that Camille may have done, but we will move forward. Let's meet back here tomorrow morning at nine a.m."

Lizzie watched the others slowly get to their feet, glancing at each other but not speaking. They made their way to the vans, loaded up their equipment, and then they headed back to the hotel.

"How are we going to accomplish this, Trisha? I don't have the slightest idea how to direct a film crew. I know how to host the show, and I know how to do the interviews, but the technical stuff is above and beyond me."

"Well, I know how to put it all together. I can handle that end of it, but we need somebody who can give us direction as a director would. Somebody who will see the things that you and I miss."

The two friends stayed quiet as they tried to think of who could come in and pitch hit as director. A few moments passed, and they both cracked grins, both knowing what the other was thinking.

"It's a perfect solution, and I know she's not busy with the galleries-its open and she's been taking it easy; this would be a perfect getaway for her." Trisha was the first to speak.

"I know she'll jump in to help. We've always had each other's back, from college on."

"So, we agree?"

They both beamed and shouted "Piper Avery" in unison.

Chapter 15

Emma looked back at the sound of Lizzie and Trisha's shout. It took a moment to connect the name of Piper Avery, but when she did, she smiled.

"If they're planning on calling in Piper, then it is a shame my mom isn't around. The four of them were quite the team. Too bad Mom's traveling with her new husband. She won't be happy to find that she's missing out on the fun." Emma gave a shrug and watched as the two older women raced back into the house to call their friend. Then Emma looked around her carefully, noting who was left in the area. The timing couldn't have been better, and she picked up her speed and raced toward the last van waiting to leave. She came to a stop and grabbed Kelly's arm, pulling her out of the van.

"Kelly, I've got that book you wanted to look at. I can give you a ride to the hotel later."

Kelly gave her a puzzled look, but when Emma gave a slight nod of her head toward her cabin, she caught on quickly.

"If you don't mind, that would be great." She turned to Tony, who was in the driver's seat of the van. "Don't worry about me, Tony. I'll get a ride back into town."

"Sure, no problem, have a good time, girls," with a wave of his hand, Tony put the van in gear, backed out of the parking spot, and headed toward the main entrance. Emma and Kelly waited until he was a safe distance away, and then Emma led the way down a secluded path.

"Wait. Aren't we going to your cabin?"

"We are, but by taking this path, everybody will think we're going to the greenhouses. We can cut off the path when we're out of sight and hike a little to my cabin. Good thing you're wearing sneakers and not sandals. We'll be going through some rough underbrush."

"Are you sure about this?"

"Look, right now, the safest place for you to be is here on the plantation, and nobody ever bothers me at the cabin. I come and go as I want and take my meals at the main house. I won't make today look any different. Let's get you settled in first, and then I'll act like you left with the others and go about my normal routine."

"You know you don't have to do this. Aren't you setting yourself up for trouble?"

"Kelly, you need help. And going back to town with that group when one of them could be a murderer just doesn't make sense. This is the safest place for you right now." Emma's tone didn't invite any arguments, not that Kelly had any to offer. She was grateful Emma was taking her in and giving her a secure place to stay.

The two girls silently made their way through the underbrush, coming around the back side of Emma's cabin. They had deliberately kept silent, not wanting their voices to carry just in case anybody was out walking the path in the garden. Once they were inside the cabin, Emma quickly closed the curtains and grabbed a pad of paper and pen that had been sitting on the makeshift desk.

"Here," she said stuffing them in Kelly's hands, "you stay here and keep quiet and out of sight. I'm going back the same way we came, and I'll go about my daily did routine. Nobody will connect that you are here, because I will not be."

"What do you want me to do with this pad of paper?"

"Write everything you can think of about the people you work with. Especially Camille. Remember, one of them is a murderer, so don't let friendship cloud your judgment. Be objective, and just write as many facts as you can. Eventually, we're going to have to let Lizzie and Trisha and Kevin in on this. But if we have enough information to give them, maybe they won't be so mad."

"Do you really think one of them is the killer?"

"Well, somebody killed Camille. And I can't picture any of the guests staying on the plantation doing it. This was something that was done in a fit of anger. It wasn't preplanned. Quite the opposite; it was done by a very optimistic opportunist." Kelly's eyes had gotten wider as Emma spoke, the realization finally sinking in that she'd been working with a killer. Not that she couldn't understand it. There were a lot of times when she would've liked to hurt Camille, but she didn't think anybody she worked with would ever go through with it.

Emma did as she said and a short time later, she was opening the back door to the plantation house, looking for Trisha and Lizzie. She wasn't sure if she was supposed to be working, but she had a feeling she was going to get the rest of the afternoon off just like everybody else.

"Where is everyone?" she asked Nora, who was standing by the kitchen sink.

"As far as I know, Kevin took off with the detective. I haven't seen hide nor hair of him. Lizzie and Trisha are over at Lizzie's talking to Piper, planning for Piper to show up here tomorrow and take over supervising the film crew." Nora paused a moment and looked at Emma. "Have you had lunch at or at least something to snack on? You've had quite a morning."

"You could say that again. Finding a body in the pond was not how I expected my day to go." Emma grimaced as she answered and shook her head, showing she had had nothing to eat. It was all Nora needed to hear, and she quickly set about making the young woman a sandwich and pouring a large glass of milk.

"You sit down at the table and get some food in you. Lizzie and Trisha will show up when they're done. I'm sure tomorrow is going to be an interesting day."

"I'd place money on that!"

Emma raised her glass of milk in a mock toast and grinned back at Nora.

EMMA SPENT THE REST of the day acting normal. As suspected, she'd been given the afternoon off with instructions that they would start first thing in the morning. Emma wandered over to the kitchen and hovered around the chef as he was making deserts for dinner, pretending she was trying to learn some new cooking skills. But she was also using the opportunity to sneak some food back to Kelly to be sure the young girl had something to eat. Other than that, she did everything she could to stay away from her cabin.

The last group of guests were sitting down to eat their dinner, and Emma had found a quiet spot in the sitting room, her headphones on, listening to a podcast of one of her favorite mysteries.

The front door opened, and the reporter, Kate, stood hesitantly on the threshold, looking around for Lizzie. Emma noticed her movements and then saw Lizzie come to the front to welcome her guest. From the angle Emma was sitting, she wasn't seen from the front door, and Lizzie didn't notice her as she led Kate across the room to sit on the couch close enough for Emma to hear their conversation. She left the headphones on, but she turned the volume down and with one finger moved the headphones slightly off her ear. Emma wasn't prone to eavesdropping, but she was curious. In the past, Lizzie and Kate barely tolerated each other, and now they were acting like coconspirators.

"I wonder what this is all about?" she thought to herself.

A few seconds later, Trisha and Kevin appeared. Kate always seemed to flirt outrageously with Kevin, but tonight she seemed to have other things on her mind and merely said hello to him. That alone aroused suspicion in Emma's mind. She shifted slightly in her seat to be sure that she could hear the conversation. And then wished she hadn't.

"I promised you I'd start looking into the backgrounds of Camille and her staff." Kate started the conversation as she opened the electronic tablet that sat on her lap.

"Did you find anything interesting?" Emma heard Lizzie ask.

"Quite the opposite. I found nothing about the staff. Except for one person, and there was very little to find about Camille. It was as if none of them existed five years ago."

"Which staff member did you find information about?" Kevin said, leaning forward, his elbows resting on his knees.

"You're not going to like it, but the person I found information about was Kelly Sky."

Emma stifled the exclamation that wanted to pop out of her mouth. The whole idea had been for Kelly to be kept under the radar, but that didn't look like it was going to work. She pushed the earphones farther off her ear to be sure she didn't miss a thing and then listened intently as Kate explained what she had found.

"First off, before I go any further, because of what I found out, I'm obligated to report it. I haven't done that yet. I'm willing to hold off until the morning because I wanted you guys to know first."

"She's just a kid. What could she possibly have done that is so awful?" interrupted Trisha not bothering to lower her voice.

"That's the thing, Trish, she's still a child. If it hadn't been for a teacher that took an interest in her, she never would have been reported as a runaway. She's been in the foster system most of her life. At ten, she started running away, almost as if she knew she was past the age of adoption and had given up. Kelly is an expert at flying below the radar and keeping invisible. For the last six years, she's been in and out of different homes, never fitting in."

"Sixteen? Are you sure?" asked Kevin, horrified. "Camille told me she was eighteen when I asked. She certainly looks eighteen."

"Yeah, well, either Kelly had some superbly forged documents or Camille had her own reasons for not turning the girl in. But either way, I have to notify social services."

Emma listened as Trisha asked more questions, not noticing that Lizzie had been quiet. But when Lizzie spoke up, Emma breathed a sigh of relief.

"Since she's involved in a murder investigation, maybe I can work with the detective, and we can figure out some way to help Kelly without sending her immediately back into the clutches of social services."

Emma watched Lizzie reach over and tap on Kate's tablet for emphasis before she spoke. "Can you hold off on reporting it until late tomorrow morning? That will give me some time to work on what we can do to help Kelly."

"Absolutely. I've dealt with enough kids that have been in this situation. It can seem pretty hopeless for them. So, if we can figure out a way to help, I'm all for it." Kate made a movement of her hand on the tablet and then looked at the surrounding three friends. "Okay, this is what I found out about Camille..."

Emma wasn't interested in hearing what they found out about Camille. She needed to get back to her cabin and talk to Kelly. And this time, she wanted the truth from the young girl.

Chapter 16

As Kate unfolded what information she had found, Lizzie's attention was drawn to the lounge chair over in the corner. The chair was situated so that the back was facing the main room, giving whomever was sitting in it privacy as well as obscuring their view. She stared at the chair for a moment but saw no movement and heard no noises and put it down to just her imagination. Her attention was brought back to Kate when the reporter made a comment about Camille.

"From what I've heard from others in the industry, Camille's company produces good work. But there seems to be an underlying tone of not wanting to work with the company a second time."

"Well, I can't say this surprises me, not after one day working with Camille. It's not a pleasant experience, and she's not the most, or rather, she wasn't the most congenial person to work with." Trisha gave a mock shudder as she agreed with what Kate had reported. Kevin shook his head, hesitated, and then spoke.

"If I'd known we were going to have so many problems, I would've just urged us to postpone the filming."

"That's easy to say in hindsight, Kevin. But you know as well as I do, we're on a tight schedule, and you can't play with the release dates of the segments. It will all get worked out." Lizzie grinned at the others before she continued, "Trisha and I have called in reinforcements."

Kevin looked up at her, surprised, and waited for an explanation. Lizzie grinned at him, knowing he was going to groan before she even finished speaking. "We've convinced Piper Avery to come up from down South and help us for a couple of days. It'll be just like our college days."

"Please tell me you don't have Megan coming as well." Kevin let out the groan at the reference to their fourth college roommate, the one who was always at the heart of trouble that the four girls would get into. Kevin had spent many weekends visiting the girls in college and had been a firsthand observer of their antics. It put the trouble that he, Lizzie, and Trish got into as teenagers into perspective; they had been amateurs.

"Unfortunately, Megan's traveling with her new husband, so we couldn't make it a full reunion, but I think the three of us will put this shoot on the right track and have plenty of time to catch up," Trisha answered for Lizzie, grinning at her best friend.

Kate watched the exchange, interested in who this new woman coming into the group would be. Then she tapped on her tablet, bringing everybody's attention back to the here and now.

"Like I said, I couldn't find any information on the rest of Camille's staff, but the information I found on Camille does not shed a very pleasant light on her. I would say she was a manipulator, and I have a feeling her staff stayed with her, not out of love for their job or to please Camille, but because they were forced to."

The three friends turned their attention to Kate, listening as she gave a few examples. They spent the next fifteen minutes going over the few notes that she had. During that time, Harry seemed to be occupied with something over in the corner, and Lizzie kept sending him warning glances. But before she could get up to see what the cat was getting into, Kate moved and dropped her tablet. While everybody's attention was diverted, Harry left the corner and walked over to join them.

"What are you up to, you troublemaker?"

Lizzie whispered as she scratched him behind the ears. But Harry didn't answer. Instead, his attention was diverted to the front door that had just opened and closed. He skirted away from Lizzie's outstretched hand and raced to the small window next to the door to look out. Lizzie got to her feet and slowly followed, looking out a higher window to see what had attracted his attention. But all she could see was a dim figure moving down the path.

"Oh Harry, it's just somebody going for a walk, probably guests that ate too much and need to walk off their dinner." Lizzie chuckled at the nosiness of the cat and then walked back toward the others. But they were wrapping things up. Kate had nothing more to add but agreed to keep looking.

"I'll hold off on calling social services until late morning. But I think you should call the police and let them know what's going on. Kelly isn't just a runaway; she's involved in the murder which makes the police involved." Kate stuck her tablet and notes back into her tote bag and got to her feet as she spoke.

"I appreciate you holding off. I'll call the detective tonight and let him know what we discovered and see what he suggests. The last thing I want to do is throw Kelly to the wolves," Lizzie said.

"Well, at least we know she's safe in her hotel room tonight, so we don't have to worry about her," added Kevin.

By mutual agreement, Kevin and Trisha left with Kate, and the three of them walked to the front door, Lizzie behind thanking them once again. Harry was winding himself amongst everybody's footsteps. He was trying to get their attention, or he was trying to give them a trip. Lizzie shooed him away. She walked out onto the porch and watched her three guests heading to the parking lot. A few moments later, car headlights shone across the lawn, and one by one, the cars backed out and headed to the main entry.

"Meow!"

Harry's insistent voice was followed by the swipe of one of his paws. Thankfully, he kept his claws sheathed, but his intention was clear: he wanted Lizzie's attention.

"What's up, Harry? You're acting kinda weird tonight."

But Harry merely howled again and then took off down the porch steps toward the pathway to the gardens. He took about ten steps and then turned back to Lizzie and howled, clearly wanting her to follow him.

Chapter 17

Harry led the way through the dim light across the lawn toward the pathways to the gardens and cabins. He didn't hesitate; he knew who he was following and didn't have a problem finding his way. His keen eyesight had adjusted to the low light. Lizzie followed at a slower pace, not wanting to trip over a stray tree limb that might have fallen on the path. The sound of mosquitos buzzing around her head made her keep a steady pace; the moment she slowed down, the insects would take advantage and attack. As they progressed, she could tell they were heading to Emma's cabin.

Lizzie expected to see Emma on the porch. The younger woman often spent her evenings reading and enjoying the evening delights of the gardens. But she wasn't expecting to find she had company, and she stopped short at the stairs to the cabin, staring at the sight in front of her. Lizzie wasn't sure who was more surprised; her or Emma. But before she could say a word, Harry pushed his way past Emma and walked right over to the chair that Kelly was sitting on. Without an invitation, he jumped up on her lap and rubbed his head on her chin.

"I can explain, Lizzie," Emma backed away from the door to allow Lizzie into the cabin.

"I hope it's a good explanation, because we all thought Kelly was safely in a hotel. What were you two thinking? There's a killer loose in the area. I don't think he's here on the property, but why would you take such a chance?"

The young women exchanged a glance, and Emma gave a slight shrug. Whether it was from embarrassment or because she had nothing to say, Lizzie didn't know, and she would not wait around to find out. Not only had the two of them found Camille's body positioning them in the center of the investigation, but Lizzie also remembered what Kate had said about Kelly.

"I think the two of you had better start talking. And I don't want any fabrications. I want the truth, and let's start with Kelly. Why are you hiding out here? Did you think nobody would notice that you're a runaway or that you're not the eighteen-year-old you pretend to be?"

Kelly hung her head for a moment and then drew in a deep breath and stood looking directly at Lizzie.

"Yes, I knew eventually it would come out. And if Camille hadn't died, I think I would've had more time working to save up more money. Because that's what this is all about, trying to get enough money to be on my own."

"Kelly, there are more important things right now to worry about than that. Why didn't you let somebody know, at the very least, you are staying here?"

"Umm, that was my idea. Kelly hadn't killed Camille because she was with me, and it seemed the safest thing would be to stay with me. I pretended I was going to take her to the hotel, and instead, I hid her out here in the cabin all day. I'm really sorry, Lizzie, for taking advantage of you. But we haven't been goofing off all day. We've been going over each of the employees of Camille's, writing everything we know about them, hoping to help you find her killer."

"This information has to go to the police. I can't be involved in another investigation like this. I promised Kevin I wouldn't." Lizzie shook her head as she muttered.

"But you already are. I heard you and Kate talking with Kevin and Trisha. That sounded very much like you were investigating the murder."

Lizzie looked at Emma and remembered the movement in the green chair while she had been sitting with the others. She hesitated a moment and then grinned back at the girl.

"I forgot how much like your mother you are. How long were you sitting there listening to us?"

"I wasn't deliberately eavesdropping. I was there first, and you all came into the room and just started talking. I was going to make myself known, but it just was too interesting, and I needed to know what Kate had found out."

Lizzie looked back and forth between the two girls. She decided they knew well enough the danger they'd put themselves in, and there was no need to continue to nag them about it.

Instead, she crossed her arms across her chest and waited. When they said nothing, she prompted the direction of the conversation.

"Show me what you came up with about the other employees that you work with, Kelly. Maybe if we have some information to give the police, it will work to your benefit."

"You're going to tell the police about me? All they are going to do is ship me back to another home." It was easy to hear the despair in her voice, but Lizzie just gave her an encouraging smile.

"Our hands are tied because of your age. We have to. But I'm working on a plan to keep you here on the plantation. And I'm going to need a lot of assurances from both of you that there's going to be no more of these shenanigans."

As Lizzie spoke, she realized she hadn't completely thought her options out, but this seemed to be the best one. They could keep an eye on Kelly if she stayed on the plantation away from the other employees. And Detective Mendoza could also monitor her, knowing where she was. If they sent her back, there was a high probability she'd run away again. Lizzie planned on using these facts when she talked to the social worker the next day. She was also going to twist the detective's arm to ensure that he would support her plan.

Emma and Kelly were nodding their heads in agreement, both assuring Lizzie with rushed voices that they would do whatever they were asked to do, wanting to give her their complete cooperation. Lizzie looked around the cabin and saw that Emma had let Kelly get comfortable. She had taken over the second bunk and had borrowed a comfortable pair of sweats and a T-shirt from Emma to wear. Making a quick decision, Lizzie turned and closed the door behind her.

"The smartest thing we can do right now is go over those notes you came up with. Emma, it looks like you got yourself a couple of guests for the night. Harry and I will stay here, where I can keep an eye on you both."

Lizzie had expected the two girls to argue, but they surprised her by quickly agreeing. It was obvious they realized they were in over their heads and welcomed adult help.

Chapter 18

Lizzie was the first one to be up the next morning, although it wasn't by choice. The solid weight of Harry jumping on her chest was her alarm clock, and as she opened her eyes, he twitched his whiskers in a self-satisfied way. Giving a groan, Lizzie pushed him off her chest and sat up. Looking across the room, she saw the two younger girls were still sleeping in that careless way of youth. Emma was curled up in a ball, hugging the pillow, but Kelly was sprawled across the bunk, her leg hanging off from under the covers, one arm tangled in her hot pink hair.

Quietly getting up to allow the girls a few more minutes of sleep, Lizzie padded to the bathroom and, when she had finished, went to the kitchen and rummaged until she found the makings for coffee. There was no way she was going to wait until they went to the main house. She needed coffee now.

While she waited for the beverage to brew, she sent off a few texts. The first one was to the detective letting him know what was going on, and the second was to Kevin informing him that his intern had smuggled Kelly into her cabin, and the young film crew member was not in the hotel as they had thought.

The smell of fresh coffee brought the girls to consciousness, and they stumbled their way to the kitchenette, rubbing the sleep out of their eyes and pushing their hair off their foreheads.

"Is smells wonderful. Thanks, Lizzie," Emma sniffed as she spoke. Kelly said nothing until after she'd taken her first sip of coffee, after Lizzie had poured the three of them each a cup.

"The nectar of the gods." She sighed with exaggeration.

After they had finished about half a cup of coffee, Lizzie cleared her throat and looked sternly at the two girls.

"I've heard from the sheriff and from Kevin. The two of you are to remain here in the cabin until they both have time to talk to you. They'll be here long before the rest of the film crew, so you don't have to worry about anyone thinking you're being singled out by the sheriff, Kelly."

The two girls looked like they were ready to argue, but one stern look from Lizzie eliminated any attempts at changing her mind and they fell silent.

"I'm going to go back over to the old house and get Harry a proper breakfast. After you talk to the police and Kevin, make your way over to the production area. My reinforcement should be up here midmorning."

"Did Piper agree to come?" Emma asked.

"Yes, we were lucky she's got a lull in the gallery and had time to fit us in. Kelly, you're in for a treat. Piper is a dream to work with, and I think you'll find her different from Camille." Lizzie smiled at the younger girl and reached out to push the hair out of her eyes. "We'll work this out, Kelly. Don't worry so much. I'll see the two of you later."

A few moments later, Lizzie nudged Harry out the front door and headed down the path toward the Higgins House. Once Harry realized he could not go back and mooch off the girls, he raced ahead, leading the way.

Lizzie herself almost turned around when she got close to the house and saw the figure sitting on her front porch. Harry simply growled and slunk around the stairs so he could inspect the scents from the intruder.

"Freddie! What are you doing here?"

"I just stopped by to see how things were going with your new project out here. I wasn't aware you lock the doors now."

Lizzie gave him a funny look and ran up the last two stairs and went directly to the front door. She turned the handle with ease and pushed open the door.

"As you can see, Freddie, I don't lock my doors. Although maybe I should start," she added under her breath.

"That door was locked. I tried with all my might to turn that knob, and it wouldn't budge. It felt like somebody was holding it in place. You have a funny way of making people feel welcome, Lizzie."

"I'm sorry you didn't feel welcome, Freddie, but I think maybe you should call and let me know you're coming, especially considering what's going on out here. Between film crews and police investigations, I'm thinking it is a good idea to keep my door locked." She gave her cousin a no-nonsense look, and crossed her arms over her chest, not inviting him inside. "Now, what can I do for you, Freddie?"

"Well, like I said, I just came out to see how things were going. Aren't you going to invite me in?"

Lizzie sighed, knowing full well Freddie wasn't here just for a visit. He was here to snoop. He had it in his head that there was a clue to the family treasures somewhere here in the original house of the old plantation. But Lizzie would not give him a chance to snoop. And this was her home now, and the last thing she wanted was her cousin starting trouble.

"You know, Freddie, I've got a really busy morning with a lot to do. Why don't you head over to the main house, and the chef can get you breakfast? There's nothing going on in this house that needs your attention. Heck, I don't even have all my furniture in yet. We're spending all of our time outside."

Freddie sputtered and looked frustrated, but there wasn't much he could do but follow Lizzie's suggestion. After a few more attempts at getting information from Lizzie in a roundabout, not-so-subtle way, he finally gave in and took her advice. He headed down the front porch steps to the path leading to the main house. As he walked away, he looked over his shoulder several times as if to see whether Lizzie was still standing by the door. She was—and she would not budge until she was sure he was at the main house.

"You're going to be a pain in my side over this, aren't you, Freddie?" she murmured to herself. "I wish everybody would just forget about that family treasure. It's long gone. Too many generations have looked for it and found nothing, me included." She chuckled to herself and then walked into the house, shutting the door firmly behind her.

As she walked toward the kitchen to give Harry his breakfast, she saw a figure dart away from the kitchen. It was the same figure she'd seen with Nora. The same figure that had given Freddie a hard time. Lizzie grinned openly, figuring out that the specter had held that door shut on Freddie. As she watched the figure disappear, she called out to where she had seen it blend into the wall.

"Thanks for the help with my cousin. You're welcome to stay here as long as you want if you can keep Freddie out of my hair."

Lizzie's laughter was met with a swirl of dust that seemed to take the shape of a laughing face. It was obvious the second ghost had a sense of humor.

Turning around in the hallway, Lizzie held her arms open wide. "Elizabeth, I hope you feel as welcome in this home as I do. You and whoever you bring with you."

The breeze fluttered from an open window, and Lizzie watched the distinct pink petals of azaleas float in through the window on the breeze.

HARRY'S INSISTENT MEOW from the kitchen reminded Lizzie of what she was supposed to be doing.

"I'm coming, Harry. You don't have to act like you're starving." With a laugh, Lizzie picked up her pace, and a few minutes later put a bowl of fresh food on the floor for Harry to indulge in.

Dropping her tote bag she was still carrying on the counter, Lizzie reached inside and pulled out the notebook Emma and Kelly had been working on when she arrived.

"While you're eating that, Harry, I'm going to make copies of the girls' work. I know I have to turn this over to the detective when he arrives, but there's no reason I can't have access to the information." Lizzie grinned as she flipped the pages, well aware that she was playing with fire. Detective Mendoza was not going to be pleased when he discovered he would have to get the notebook from her. Lizzie had instructed Emma and Kelly to tell the detective everything, including the information in the notebook. She wasn't trying to hide the information from him, she just wanted a copy for herself. She looked at things a little differently than the detective did. He had to look at things as either black or white, based on the facts as they were presented. Lizzie knew from experience a lot of grays could mix in with black and white, and this was where the most interesting questions and answers would be found.

Knowing she didn't have much time, Lizzie walked into her office next to the kitchen. It used to be a large screen porch but had been converted into a Florida room with roll-up windows that let in lots of sunshine and comfortable wicker furniture. One corner of the room had been designated as her office. In true teacher fashion, she had a large chalkboard and some filing cabinets. Her computer and printer sat on an oversized desk that had been in the house from the beginning. More than once, Lizzie had looked at the desk, wondering which of her relatives had used it in the past. Laying the notebook on the screen of the printer, she meticulously copied each page. As the pages printed, she took them to the chalkboard and secured them in place to study at length. Remembering Freddie, she made a mental note to herself to make sure the office was locked when she wasn't around. She did not want any innocent persons to be caught up in Camille's death by somebody carelessly seeing this evidence.

Taking the last piece of paper to the chalkboard, she took a step back and looked at it. The girls had written on each page the name of Kelly's co-workers and a few sentences about each. Under each name, the girls had come up with a catchphrase. She was impressed to say they had also included a page for Camille and Kelly as well. This showed Lizzie that Kelly wasn't trying to hide anything. Walking closer to the board, she looked at Camille's page first.

"*Secret keeper.* That's an interesting tagline. Not one I would expect from her. I would have thought something more like a commander or tyrant." Lizzie rubbed her chin as she studied the phrase. There were a few other things under the tagline, but they weren't what caught her interest.

Deciding the two girls were quite insightful with their taglines, she went to the next one and concentrated on what they had to say about Tony.

The Great Pretender. Lizzie wrinkled her brow as she thought about that one. Tony seemed openly flamboyant in his personality, and she couldn't imagine him pretending to be anything.

Next in line was Tiffany Stone, and her tagline read, *Wannabe.*

"I don't know girls. I think most people would want to be Tiffany. She seems to have it made." Lizzie spoke out loud, wondering about the girls' reasoning.

Earl Chambers was next in line, and Kelly had not only written *Puppy Dog*, but she had drawn a cute little puppy dog face with long floppy ears and a tongue hanging out of his mouth. While there was no guessing what she meant by that. Lizzie remembered several people mentioning Earl followed Camille from site to site like some sort of groupie.

The last person was Ophelia Michaels. Lizzie put her hand on her hips and tilted her head as she studied the paperwork. She couldn't imagine what the girls had thought of as a tagline for this one. She was afraid of her own shadow. But just like with Earl, they came up with one word along with a picture. A little field mouse was sniffing at the word *Mouse* on the paper.

"Kelly, you've got some talent there, as well as a snarky sense of humor." Lizzie murmured out loud as she looked at Kelly's illustrations.

Lizzie looked at the last paper to take to the blackboard and found Kelly had written nothing other than the word Runaway, so there was no getting any additional information that Lizzie didn't already know.

Those were the suspects that the girls had concentrated on, and Lizzie agreed with their assessment. These were the primary suspects that needed the attention of the investigators, whether it be the lawful investigators or the nosy ones.

Chapter 19

Lizzie was lost in thought as she pondered the pages taped to the chalkboard and the names the girls had given each of the suspects. It wasn't until she felt something soft and cushy rub against her ankle that she came back to the present.

"What's your insight on this matter, Harry?" Lizzie bent down and picked up the cat and took a step closer to the chalkboard. Harry reached out his paw and tapped on the picture of the field mouse.

Is that your prime suspect, or are you just in the mood to chase a mouse?"

Harry turned his head just enough to look at Lizzie in the eye and twitched his whiskers. Then he turned his attention back to the papers. Lizzie moved a couple of inches so he could have more access to the paperwork. She didn't know if she was serious or not, but Harry seemed to have an opinion, and she wanted to hear it.

Harry was silent for a moment, and then a low growl started deep in his throat, building up to a howl that resonated in her ears. She looked at the cat, wondering what was going on, to find him staring at one page. Before she could say anything, there was a loud knocking on the kitchen door, and Harry jumped from her arms and ran to hide behind the desk.

"Did that howl mean something other than somebody was at the door, Harry?" Lizzie didn't wait to see if the cat was going to answer, and she made her way to the kitchen. The door opened, admitting Emma and Kelly with the tall figure of Detective Mendoza standing behind them. The detective did not look to be in a good mood.

"Come on in, everyone. Detective, have you had your morning coffee yet?" Lizzie asked cordially, but the detective ignored her offer of coffee and got right to the point.

"I understand the girls gave you a notebook with information about Camille and the other staff members. I would like it. Now."

Lizzie hid her smile. She was right. The detective was not amused that she had taken the notebook.

"Of course, you want it. Emma, pour the detective a cup of coffee while I get the notebook."

Lizzie didn't give the detective the opportunity to argue and hurried back to her office, where she grabbed the notebook. She wanted to hand it to him in the kitchen and not have him follow her to her office, where he would see that she had made copies.

By the time Lizzie returned to the kitchen, the detective was sitting at the table stirring the sugar into his coffee while the two younger girls sat across the table from him, watching his every movement. Walking across the room, Lizzie placed the notebook on the table next to the detective, giving him a cheerful smile.

"I don't know what you read in that notebook, Lizzie, but you may as well forget about it now. You're not getting involved in this. I just need to ask you a few more questions, and then your involvement in this is over."

Lizzie smiled at the detective and took the seat next to him, giving all appearances of being cooperative.

I wouldn't bet on it; she thought behind her smile.

"Other than the note you saw Camille throw away, did she seem at all preoccupied or afraid of anything yesterday?" The detective jumped right into his questioning, not wasting any time. Lizzie had a feeling he wanted to get the questioning over with so he could push her back under the rug and not have to deal with her for the rest of the investigation. With a sweet smile, she cooperated with him, even if she had no intention of dropping her part in the investigation.

"Well, first off, you have to understand, I just met Camille yesterday. I'd never seen or heard of her before. I can't say that she made a wonderful impression on me, but she seemed competent, and I would say unafraid of anything."

"Did she seem afraid after she read the note?"

"No," Lizzie gave a short laugh. "If anything, she seemed angry about it—angry and annoyed."

"Did you notice if anybody else was watching her movements to see how she would react to the note?"

Lizzie thought for a moment, remembering the actions of the others, then she gave a slow shake of her head.

"I don't think so. Everybody seemed intent on doing their job."

As Lizzie spoke, the detective was turning the pages in the notebook. He looked up sharply at Emma and Kelly.

"You two seem pretty observant about the people you are working with. But I need to ask you about this one."

Three pairs of eyes were riveted to the page that the detective was pointing at. It was Kelly's page, and the detective's finger was tapping on the word *Runaway*.

Before Kelly could say a word, Lizzie spoke up.

"Detective, I realize with Kelly being a minor, we have to notify social services. However, with your endorsement, I would like to suggest that Kelly stay here at Azalea Plantation rather than going with a social service agent to wherever they would take her. We can monitor and keep her safe. She can keep working under our supervision."

Detective Mendoza gave a nod, and then a smile spread across his face.

"For once, you and I are in full agreement. I was going to suggest the same thing. If I know where Ms. Sky is, I can protect her easier."

"Do you really think I'm in danger?" Kelly interrupted before the detective could finish, her eyes darting between the two adults as if she was realizing just what her position was.

"There's a killer on the loose, Miss Sky. As far as I'm concerned, everyone's in danger. But I also want things to run as if Camille was still in charge. When things go about as normal, a killer will make a mistake becoming overconfident that he or she is going to get away with the crime." The detective paused and looked at Lizzie. "You do plan on continuing your filming project, don't you?"

"Yes, I have somebody coming up to help oversee the project, but I will continue to use Camille's crew to get the work done."

"Perfect." The detective snapped the notebook closed and got to his feet. "I'll contact social services and arrange to meet with them later today. In the meantime, I will post one or two officers out here to continue to gather evidence and for protection."

The detective looked at the two younger women and smiled reassuringly, then he looked at Lizzie and frowned.

"I've put you right back in the middle of the investigation, haven't I?"

Wisely, Lizzie said nothing in return, but she didn't need to; the grin on her face said it all. Swallowing a groan, the detective made his way to the back door. At the same time he was opening it, a woman of Lizzie's age with long silver hair was raising her hand to knock.

"Piper!" Lizzie squealed like a schoolgirl.

Chapter 20

The detective left the kitchen with barely a noticeable acknowledgment. The women in the kitchen were too busy greeting Lizzie's old college roommate, introducing Kelly, and filling Piper in on the recent events. As he walked down the stairs, he could hear the women talking, and he gave a sigh. Was the sigh because he was relieved to not be trapped in the kitchen with all the female chatter, or because of the workload ahead of him?

It didn't take long for the introductions to be completed, and Piper was astounded. She had her own brushes with murder, and it appalled her this happened in such a beautiful location as Azalea Plantation.

"Well, I know you, Lizzie, and you're not going to just sit around while something like this is going on around you. Between Trisha and me, you don't have to worry about what's going on with the shoot. And if you need any help with your extracurricular activities, let me know."

"Thanks, Piper. No, you're here to take care of filming the show segment. And that is an enormous weight off my shoulders. I think the fewer people that are involved in trying to find out what happened to Camille, the better. Detective Mendoza is not the most congenial person when he feels you're treading on his investigation. To be honest, the only reason I can get away with it is because he and Kevin are such good friends." Lizzie shared a laugh with Piper and then looked out the kitchen door to see Trisha walking up the stairs.

"Trisha, come on in. Piper is already here." She called out through the open screen door, and Trisha picked up her pace.

Trisha and Piper needed no time to catch up. They had been talking on the phone and knew what was going on in each other's life. Their concentration had to be on the filming.

"The rest of the film crew should be here in about ten minutes. Why don't you and I go down and walk through the area to get a feel for it?" Trisha linked arms with Piper and led her friend out the door. As they bent their heads to talk over their plans for the shoot, Lizzie turned to the younger girls with a stern look.

"I want the two of you to stick together like glue today and remember to stay in sight of other people. I don't know if Camille's death is the end of this situation, but I don't want either of you to be in danger. Keep your eyes and ears open, and frankly, your mouth shut."

Kelly silently nodded, relieved that she wasn't getting shipped off to social services right away. Emma felt protective of the younger girl and agreed with Lizzie's assessment.

"Don't worry about us. We'll look out for each other. Is there anything special you want us to listen for?"

"Emma, just keep your ears open. In a situation like this, gossip will run rampant. I don't know how much of that will be speculation and how much of that will be true, but we need to monitor all of it. If you hear anything that sounds out of the ordinary and might be useful, let me know right away."

Harry jumped up on the counter and let out a meow, as if he was adding his own caution to Kelly and Emma. Kelly reached out and gave him a scratch under the chin, and Emma reached over and snatched one of his treats out of the jar and gave it to him.

"No wonder that cat never loses any weight," Lizzie groaned, and they all laughed.

Looking at the door, Lizzie noticed the two vans driving up the driveway and heading toward the parking area she had designated for the film crew. It was time to get to work.

The morning went smoothly. It started out quiet, as if everyone was afraid to talk, but slowly, as they got into their routine and became familiar with Piper, the gossip began. Even Lizzie could catch it, because nobody was trying to be discreet.

"I can't say I'm surprised she's gone. That woman went out of her way to be nasty and mean to people," Tiffany said.

But Earl quickly reprimanded her. "Camille wasn't a bad person. She just liked to find out about people and keep them close to her."

"Is that what you call it?" Tony gave a loud bark of laughter, shaking his head in disbelief.

It was Ophelia who had the burning question that no one could answer.

"I packed everything up yesterday. I found Camille's tablet and notebook, but I can't find her phone anywhere. Has anybody seen it? I know she has notes on it about the shoot."

One by one, they all said they had not seen it, not since watching Camille walk away toward the van, the phone in her hand.

I wonder what else Camille had on that phone. Lizzie thought and couldn't help noticing the tension within the group intensifying with Ophelia's announcement that the phone was missing.

Lizzie closely watched the interaction between the film crew. The one thing she noticed was nobody seemed to miss Camille. If anything, her name wasn't even mentioned. It was almost as if they were trying to erase her from existence. Although things seemed more lighthearted, and there was much more teasing and joking than she'd seen on the set the previous day, Lizzie couldn't help noticing everybody was watching each other, each trying not to get caught spying on their co-workers.

It was hard not to watch Earl as he walked amongst the crew. He had no real reason to be there, and the others ignored him. Only Tony seemed to make biting remarks about him being a lost puppy.

"Tony, knock it off. At least somebody really was concerned about her." Lizzie heard Ophelia hissed at her co-worker as she walked by after Tony had made another nasty remark to Earl. But Tony only laughed and shrugged. He wasn't concerned about whether he hurt the man's feelings.

"Ophelia, you really can't find her phone?" Lizzie overheard Tiffany ask the other woman as they walked by. Ophelia looked around her and saw Lizzie and merely gave a shrug, not wanting to engage in conversation.

"I wonder what everybody is hiding. They're obviously concerned about that phone. And I'd like to find it as well." Lizzie had picked Harry up to get him out of the way of the cameras and whispered in his ear as the two women walked by.

Harry didn't comment, he just reached his paw and swiped at a wisp of her hair that the wind was playing with.

"I don't suppose you know where her phone is, do you, Harry?" Lizzie tilted her head as she talked to the cat, but then Earl's movements caught her attention. He was moving around some of the equipment, and Lizzie wondered what he was up to. But before she could ask, Emma and Kelly joined him and picked up a large box from where he was standing and carried it over to Piper. The older man stared at them for a moment, and Lizzie watched him shove his hands in his pockets. She couldn't help but feel sorry for the man. He had adored Camille and now seemed a little lost without her, even if all she did was snip at him and order him around.

Apparently, somebody else felt the same way, and Tiffany walked over to Earl and put her hand on his arm. She spoke to him softly, and he gave a sad smile and walked away. Tiffany looked up and saw Lizzie looking at her.

"I don't know what Earl is going to do without Camille around. He's been following her around for years."

"So, he's not part of the staff?" Lizzie asked, even though she knew the answer.

"No, he's a traditional old-fashioned groupie, and Camille was his idol. He followed us from shoot to shoot, never got paid, never asked for pay, and was happy just to be at her beck and call." Tiffany gave a short laugh and shrugged. Then she was called away by Ophelia, and they quickly dropped the subject of Earl. There was work to be done, and without Camille getting in the way, things seemed to run smoothly. So smoothly that Lizzie decided they did not need her on the site. She glanced at her watch and realized she had enough time to visit Kevin at his office before the woman from social services was supposed to meet them. She sent a quick text to the detective to remind him of the meeting and then called out to Piper and Trish.

"You guys have this under control. I'm leaving it in your hands. Call me if anything comes up. And keep an eye on those two girls." With a wave, Lizzie went back in the house to get her car keys and purse. A short time later, she was driving down the main drive toward town.

Chapter 21

As Lizzie entered the reception area of Kevin's office, she could hear male laughter coming from the direction of the conference room. Ignoring the bell on the reception desk, placed there for visitors to ring, Lizzie followed the sound of laughter and walked down the hallway conference room.

"What's up with you two? Anything new in the investigation, detective?" Lizzie announced her presence with her questions, and the two men turned to look at her, Kevin grinning broadly and the detective only giving her a half smile.

"Not much. We're going through Camille's laptop and, of course, continuing to question the suspects, but it doesn't seem like we're getting anywhere."

Lizzie was surprised that the detective gave her a straight answer. She half expected to be brushed off and told to mind her own business, but it seemed he had accepted that she was going to stick her nose into his investigation. Rather than fighting, it seemed like he was going to accept it.

"I got a text from Trisha that Piper had arrived. How's the shoot moving along?" Kevin asked.

"Smoothly. Which is nice. Piper stepped right in, and everybody loves her, of course. Between her and Trisha, they've come up with a few interesting ideas to incorporate. I think it's going to be a good segment, even better than what we originally thought."

Lizzie hesitated for a moment, thinking about what she'd observed earlier in the morning, and then she turned to the detective.

"I couldn't help overhear some whispers from Camille's crew. It seems her phone has gone missing, and for some reason, they're all a bit uptight about it."

The detective gave a nod of agreement. "That is interesting. We haven't seen her phone either, and I noted it was missing. A woman like Camille always has her phone with her, so it's either at the bottom of the pond or somebody stole it."

"Why would everybody be upset about her phone being missing?" Kevin asked.

"It's an interesting point. I would guess our victim had something on her phone the others didn't want to come out."

Kevin and Lizzie exchanged a look, knowing the detective was probably right. Then Lizzie changed the subject.

"What am I supposed to do about Earl? He's not part of the crew, and if anything, he seems to be a butt for their jokes. Do I kick him off the site or let him wander and see how it plays out?"

The detective was silent for a moment, thinking about her question. When he answered, he was looking at Kevin for agreement.

"Let things be. The more relaxed and normal it'll feel for them, the more things will slip out. And it seems Earl is normally around the site of a shoot. You okay with that, Kevin?"

"Yes, there are enough people watching that it shouldn't be a problem. And like you said, if things seem normal, the suspects may just let down their guard."

The detective took that opportunity to change subjects, and he gave Lizzie his full attention.

"I know you are sniffing around, and frankly, it doesn't matter; if you come up with something, that's fine. But you have got to give the appearance of being a calming safe influence for Kelly in order for the social service agent to agree to let her stay with you. So, while she's here, there's no talk about the murder or the suspects; there's only talk about keeping Kelly safe and how upstanding a person you are. Got it?"

Lizzie nodded, but before she could answer, the bell at the reception desk rang, and a woman's voice called out.

"Hello? Anybody here?"

Kevin jumped to his feet and headed to the reception area. A few moments later, he returned, followed by a plump rosy-cheeked woman in her early sixties. Her dark hair was cut short with curls, creating a cloud around her head in a mixture of black and silver.

"Good morning, I'm Penelope Fox from social services. I believe we have an appointment to talk about Kelly Sky."

Lizzie studied the woman silently while Detective Mendoza stood and shook her hand, introducing himself. She wasn't sure what she was expecting, but she liked the looks of Penelope. The woman gave an aura of calmness and efficiency which Lizzie had a feeling was exactly what was going to be needed to deal with Kelly.

Penelope didn't waste any time with chitchat. Instead, she took the chair Kevin offered and pulled out two folders from her briefcase. She smiled at Lizzie and then opened the folder on top. Lizzie wasn't surprised to find this was Kelly's folder, and she was pleased with the woman's efficiency.

"I understand the urgency of your investigation, Detective Mendoza. However, I need you to understand my priority is to Kelly Sky. And it doesn't look like very many people have taken her needs into consideration in the past. I intend to do something about that. The child needs to have a safe location, one she feels comfortable and secure in. Do you feel your home will offer this, Professor Higgins?"

Yes, Lizzie was going to like Penelope a lot. The woman was direct and to the point. And she seemed to be the first person in a long time who genuinely cared about what happened to Kelly.

"Kelly has already spent the night at my home, and I think she feels very comfortable. She's made friends with one of the other girls her age who is staying with me as well. Of course, the detective has patrols for security reasons, and there are plenty of my staff around to monitor the child's movements."

Penelope nodded, pleased with Lizzie's answer.

"Kelly will be your responsibility, so I want her staying in your house, not with somebody else. Thankfully, with you being in the educational system, your background checks out perfectly. That saves us a lot of time of having to do a background check, and I am very familiar with Azalea Plantation, so I feel comfortable that this would be a suitable location for the child. If the house that you're staying in is anything like the main bed-and-breakfast, I know she'll be well cared for." Penelope paused for a moment and then looked sternly at Lizzie, emphasizing her point as she tapped the file in her lap. Lizzie looked down and saw the second file had her name on it, and sure enough, Penelope had done her work and checked out Lizzie's background.

"I think we can make this work. And if it's okay with you, I would like to come out to the plantation and talk to Kelly over the next few days and assess what her needs are. They have lost her in the system for far too long. She needs my attention now, before she ages out."

Kevin had been watching the exchange and spoke up.

"She has attached herself to my intern and is a staff for the film crew. If it meets with your approval, we can continue letting her work on the set."

"It would probably be the best thing to keep her out of trouble and occupied. If she's happy, she won't make a run for it. And you, Detective Mendoza, are guaranteeing me that there will be plenty of security on-site so that I don't have to worry about her?" The detective agreed, but Lizzie wasn't sure if he was answering a question or obeying a command.

"Well, I think we have this settled, Professor Higgins. We have paperwork that we need to settle before we can go any further. If you have a moment, let's get this taken care of now. And then I'd like to come out first thing in the morning and talk to Kelly and you together."

As she spoke, Penelope pulled another file from her briefcase, grabbed a pen off of Kevin's desk and spread out the paperwork for Lizzie to read and sign.

Chapter 22

Emma looked around frantically until she located Kelly talking to Piper. Even with her bright pink hair, Kelly had a habit of disappearing from Emma's view. Being short didn't help, and she had the grace and spunk of an overzealous pixie. She wanted to know everything that was going on through the shoot and was constantly asking Piper and Trisha questions. The older women were patient, explaining everything she asked about.

"Kelly, over here! I need your help." Emma had learned quickly that the easiest way to get Kelly to stay by her side was if the younger girl thought she was being useful.

"What, Emma?" Kelly raced over to stand in front of Emma, looking around to see what Emma needed help with.

"Look, we promised Lizzie we'd stick together, and you keep running off—"

"I'm right here; it's no big deal. I'm keeping you in sight at all times. Believe me, I don't want to give you any trouble, and I sure don't want to end up like Camille."

Emma gave a shrug. She was learning there was no way to keep a constant handle on the younger girl; she was just too full of energy.

"Listen, everybody's taking a break and heading over to the bed-and-breakfast for some food. Now is the perfect time to eavesdrop and see what's going on. They seem to talk more by themselves versus being too close to Trisha and Piper."

"Yeah, I noticed that too. And basically, I'm invisible. They constantly talk in front of me without even thinking about it."

"Let's give them a couple minutes to get over and get settled, and then we'll sneak in and find a chair or table close enough to hear the conversations."

Kelly gave a nod of agreement with Emma's suggestion, and they watched as the rest of the film crew headed over to the main house. Piper and Trisha made their way into Lizzie's house rather than joining the others. The two girls waited, hearing the back door to Lizzie's house slam shut, and watched the others enter the front entrance of the plantation house. Then they raced across the lawn to the back entrance of the bed-and-breakfast. Cutting through the kitchen, they entered the dining room and spotted a table was close enough to the others that they could hear the conversation, but not be noticed. As they made their way to the table, they quickly grabbed a drink and snacks to munch on.

"Well, I have to admit Piper is a lot easier to work with than Camille." Tony stretched his arms over his head, working out the kinks from holding the camera as he spoke.

Emma grinned at Kelly. She was right; they were going to pick up on some gossip.

"Piper even has Earl feeling like he's part of the group. She sent him back into town to pick up some supplies. That's what that poor man needs, a purpose and a kind word." Ophelia said, and Tiffany nodded in agreement.

Tony didn't answer right away. He was busy taking a huge bite of the Danish he held in his hand and chased it with a swig of soda. Wiping his mouth with the back of his hand, he looked at the two sitting across from him and smirked.

"You two are too soft. Camille was right to use Earl to her advantage. If he is going to hang around all the time, why not?"

"You know as well as I do, Camille was a user, and it didn't matter who was the subject of her abuse. Frankly, I'm glad she's gone," Tiffany said.

"I have to admit it's nice not to have to look over my shoulder every five minutes and see that knowing look on Camille's face and wonder when she was going to tell my secret," Blurted Ophelia.

Tony and Tiffany looked at her, shocked. Ophelia got a funny look on her face when she realized what she had said.

"You too, huh?" Tony grunted.

"I think if we're honest, we all know Camille had something on everybody she worked with. That's the only way she can keep us working; with the threat of revealing our secrets." Tiffany picked up her drink and took a swallow, waiting to see how the others would react to her statement.

Emma leaned forward, hoping to hear more of the conversation, but it was as if the three at the other table had become lost in their own thoughts. It didn't look as if they were going to reveal what secrets Camille had on them. The moment was lost when Nora came by with a plate of cheese and crackers to set on the table. Her appearance at the girls' table drew the attention of the others, and Emma sighed. Now that the others knew they were there, their conversation turned to more general topics.

"We're not going to learn anything more here, Emma," Kelly leaned across and whispered.

Emma nodded, and the two girls finished the food in front of them without a word. Finishing her meal, Kelly got to her feet and stacked the dirty dishes on the sideboard. Then she turned to Emma and motioned with her hand for the other girl to follow her. Once they were outside, Kelly grinned at her new friend.

"We may not have gotten the details, but we got the gist of what's going on. Listen, I forgot something in your cabin. Can we run over and get it before we have to go back to work?"

"Sure, we have enough time before we have to get back, and we're not going to learn anything more here."

Full of energy, Kelly took the lead and headed down the shady trail toward Emma's cabin. As they walked, the sky became dark with clouds, and it began to sprinkle.

"I bet they cancel the rest of work for today. You can't film in this kind of weather," Emma said.

But a sudden gust of wind blew her words away from Kelly, and a large branch from one of the oak trees snapped and fell in front of them.

"Wow, that was close!" gasped Emma.

But Kelly didn't answer. Her attention was on something ahead of her, and Emma peered over her shoulder to see what was going on.

"Do you see it?" Kelly whispered, pointing off to the side.

Emma saw something, but she wasn't sure what it was. It was a shadowy figure, but Kelly seemed to see it without a problem.

"I don't think we should go to your cabin. Whatever that is in front of us wants us to follow it."

"Kelly it's probably just a shadow from the wind blowing the leaves." But Emma's voice didn't sound too sure, and Kelly turned and looked at her.

"I don't think so, Emma. It's just the feeling that I have. And these feelings have kept me out of trouble before. Whatever it is, it does not want us to go near the cabin. Come on." Without giving Emma a chance to reply, Kelly turned toward whatever she saw and started pushing her way through the undergrowth. Emma gave a quick look toward her cabin, and a shiver ran up her spine. The clouds had made it dark, and Emma could clearly see the light was on. A light that she had turned off earlier in the morning. Whatever Kelly was following was leading them away from danger and into safety, and Emma would not question it. She turned away from the cabin and followed Kelly.

They worked their way through the wild vegetation until they found a small path. From there, they hurried forward until they came to a creek that led to Lizzie's house. Somehow, they had come all the way around the back of the property and were close to the preserve where the creek divided Lizzie's property from a wildlife sanctuary. Now that they were out in the open, Kelly came to a standstill and looked around.

"Did you see her? She was beautiful and reminded me of Lizzie, except she was dressed in some really, really old clothes. But she's gone now, and I don't feel that tingling of danger anymore."

Emma looked back toward the cabin and then turned her full attention to Kelly. The girl didn't look like she was trying to pull a prank. She was deadly serious. And that's when Emma remembered the stories of the Higgins ghost.

Chapter 23

Emma looked at Kelly and simultaneously, the two girls began speaking, each trying to explain their own take on what they had seen. Still talking a mile-a-minute, they moved toward the back door of Lizzie's house, and burst through the door, their voices getting shrill with excitement and a tinge of fear.

"What's going on out here?"

The ruckus the girls were making had brought Trish and Piper from Lizzie's office, where they had been working. Piper took one look at the frazzled girls as she asked her questions and led them to the kitchen table where she sat them both down. Piper automatically went to the refrigerator and got two sodas, placing one in front of each girl. Without being told, Emma and Kelly took a swig of their drink, filling the room with sudden silence.

"Okay, what's got you so riled up?" asked Piper calmly. After raising two boys, she was well aware of how small things could get blown out of proportion.

"I think I saw a ghost!"

"Someone's in my cabin snooping!"

Both girls started talking over each other again, and Trish held up her hands for quiet.

"One at a time. Let's deal with the most pressing items first. Emma, what makes you think somebody's in your cabin?"

"Oh, I know somebody is. There's a light on in my cabin that I distinctly turned off this morning. I remember doing it because I had to put down the stuff I had in my hands in order to turn the switch. But when I looked over toward my cabin, it had gotten dark enough because of the rain that I could clearly see the light glowing in the window."

Kelly looked at Emma in surprise. She'd been so wrapped up in what she had seen she didn't realize Emma had also witnessed something out of the ordinary.

"The ghost was really trying to help us, trying to lead us to safety. I knew it!"

Emma looked at her friend and slowly nodded, realizing Kelly was probably right. Trisha caught the movement and gave Emma a direct stare.

"Did you see what Kelly was talking about?" she asked.

"I saw something, not as clearly as Kelly obviously did, but there was something motioning for us to leave the path going to the cabin. And I was just afraid enough to follow Kelly's lead and not question her. I figured a ghost would be easier to confront than a trespasser."

"Well, neither one of you can stay in the cabin tonight if somebody's nosing around. I'm going to text Josh over at the greenhouse and have him meet you at the cabin. You can grab what you need for the night, and he can check around to make sure it's safe. Then we'll lock it up and deal with this in the morning." Trisha took charge and sent a text over to the greenhouse recruiting backup and somebody to help the girls carry their stuff back to Lizzie's.

Piper caught Trisha's glance and tilted her head in question. "I've had a tour of the house. There's no furniture upstairs for anybody to sleep on. Just a blow-up bed that Lizzie's using."

Trisha tapped her finger on her chin as she thought. Then she snapped her fingers as an idea took hold and formed in her mind.

"Lizzie has most of the furniture for the upstairs suites in storage. We've just been waiting to book the movers. But I think this is an emergency and we'll have to just use the greenhouse staff and whoever's available from the bed-and-breakfast and get the stuff over here for tonight. At least enough so the girls have the bed. We can deal with the rest later. In the meantime, I need to call Lizzie and let her know what's going on. I'm sure she'll agree with whatever I plan. Piper, can you walk over with the girls and meet the greenhouse guys at the cabin?"

"Do you think it's safe to go back to the cabin?" asked Kelly, her nervousness clear in her voice.

"By the time we all get there, whoever was nosing around will have left. And we'll make enough noise as we approach the cabin to ensure if anybody is in there, they'll make a run for it," Piper reassured the young girl with a smile.

Trisha motioned for the girls to finish their soda, and then she walked back into Lizzie's office and made her phone calls.

Emma was surprised Piper didn't try to pry more information out of her. Instead, she just sat silently while the two girls finished their soda. It was the pounding on the screen door to the kitchen that made all three of them look up with a start.

"I thought maybe you could use an escort."

Josh Bennington stood on the other side of the screen, grinning at them. Emma immediately felt better knowing they would not have to walk the path back to the cabin by themselves. She had mentally been going over what she was going to take with her as a weapon for protection, but now that Josh was here, she didn't think it was necessary.

"That would be wonderful, Josh. It's good to see you. I haven't seen you in a while," Piper smiled at the younger man and opened the screen door for him to enter the kitchen. She knew most of the staff on the plantation. She had spent a lot of long weekends here with Lizzie over the years.

Josh grinned back at her in greeting and then looked at Emma and Kelly questioningly.

"Are you two sure you saw somebody in the cabin?" he asked. Emma nodded vigorously, no doubt in her mind.

"Okay, let's find out who's been snooping around." Josh's voice sounded cheerful, but it was hard not to see the serious look on his face.

Moments later, the four of them were on the path heading toward the cabin. The rain had lessened to a mere drizzle, but the skies were still dark and thick with clouds, making the path darker than normal. There was just enough wind to blow the mist from the drizzle into their faces, and the dampness from the earth mingled with the sweet smell of some wildflowers growing off the path. Now that it wasn't raining, the birds were chirping again, and everything seemed normal, but Emma knew it wasn't.

"Wait out here," Josh said when they reached the cabin. There were two other workers from the greenhouse approaching, and he motioned for them to join them. The three men entered the cabin first and then came out a few moments later.

"There's no one here."

"Good. Emma and Kelly, go in and grab the supplies you'll need for tonight and tomorrow morning, and we'll head back to Lizzie's," Piper instructed after getting a reassuring nod from the three men now standing on the porch.

"If that's all you need us for, we're going to get the delivery truck and a couple more guys and head over to the storage unit. Trish said there's stuff we need to bring back to Lizzie's and set up. Everything looks normal. There's no reason to worry," Josh said as he reassured the two girls. Piper gave a wave of her hand, signaling for the men to leave, and then stepped inside the cabin, holding the door open for Emma and Kelly.

Kelly rushed over to her pile of belongings and stuffed what she needed for the night into her backpack. Emma followed at a slower pace, her eyes darting from one corner of the room to the other, looking for anything out of place.

"Come on, Emma. It'll be dark soon, and I really don't want to walk through those paths without a flashlight." Piper tapped Emma on the shoulder, encouraging her to pick up the pace.

Emma gave a nod and quickly gathered her belongings. She was almost done when she remembered a book she wanted to finish reading, and she ran to the bedside table to grab it.

As she picked the book up and stuffed it into her backpack, she looked down at the floor and saw a white linen cloth sticking out from the corner of the table.

"What's this?" she asked herself as she leaned down and picked it up. She couldn't help but notice the richness of the cloth, more silk than linen, and the corner had a fancy logo. Not recognizing it, she stuffed it into her pocket absentmindedly and hurried back to the others. Moments later, she locked the door behind her, and they set off for Lizzie's.

Chapter 24

Lizzie stared at the phone in her hand, not knowing if she should laugh or worry.

"Anything wrong?" Kevin was sitting next to her and had been silent while she spoke on the phone with Trisha.

"I don't think there's anything seriously wrong, but things are definitely not the way it should be back at the house. Kelly is insisting she saw a ghost, and Emma is insisting that somebody was in her cabin that didn't belong. Piper is handling everything like a pro, and Trisha is wondering how she should handle the girls."

"Is that all?" Kevin laughed.

"It's a crazy farm back there. Thank goodness I got this call after Penelope and Detective Mendoza left. Otherwise, if Penelope was here, she would've walked back to the house and yanked Kelly away from us. Which is good. She definitely seems protective toward Kelly, something I don't think she's had very much of."

"Do you want to head back to the plantation and see what is going on?"

"There's really no reason to. Trisha and Piper have everything under control. Emma and Kelly are moving in with me. Oh boy."

Kevin let out a loud bark of laughter at the look on her face. It was no secret Lizzie enjoyed her privacy, and the idea of her first houseguests being two young women, one still a teenager, was amusing.

"It's not funny, Kevin," Lizzie admonished, and then joined in his laughter. "Thank goodness Trisha is organized. She's already arranged for the furniture we have in storage to be brought to the house, so the girls have beds to sleep on. Nora has taken the girls under her wing to keep them calm."

"Or will she just feed the fire? I can remember all your family ghost stories Nora used to tell us when we were growing up. I'm sure when she hears Kelly saw a ghost, she's going to fill her in on all the details."

Lizzie laughed and then remembered how calm Nora had been when the apparition had appeared in their kitchen and frightened Freddie away.

"I don't think they're just stories to Nora. I think over the years, she has had some first-hand experience herself with my family's ghosts."

"Well, that explains why she was never rattled when one of us talked about it." Lizzie slowly nodded, remembering how when she was younger, she swore she had seen the ghost on several occasions, and Nora had never dissuaded her or tried to tell her she was wrong. She simply accepted what Lizzie and her friends had said and kept them calm.

"I used to doubt whether we had really seen Elizabeth Higgins in her ghostly appearance when we were younger. But since I've moved into the plantation house, I've seen her and seen evidence of her. I'm not going to dismiss Kelly's rendition of what happened this afternoon so easily." Lizzie spoke quietly, the laughter gone from her voice.

While she was talking, Kevin had reached over to his own phone and was punching in a number. Lizzie gave him a questioning look, which he ignored. Chances were if Lizzie knew who he was calling, she would've stopped him before the phone rang on the other end. But his concern was that somebody had been in the cabin. Emma wasn't one to panic, and he knew from experience the cleaning crews only had admittance to her cabin once a week to change the sheets and do a quick cleanup. The rest was Emma's responsibility. When Lizzie heard who he was talking to, she gave a nod of approval and didn't dissuade him. A few moments later, arrangements had been made, and he hung up the phone.

"Thanks, Kevin, I should've thought of that right away. We have security in all the buildings. Of course, not inside the buildings for privacy of the guests, but I never thought to add it to the old plantation house. We'll add it, but just the external security. I don't want cameras inside my home."

"That's what I figured. And you can monitor right from your phone who comes and goes to the plantation house. I know you've never bothered before, but under the circumstances, it might not be a bad idea."

Lizzie shrugged and didn't answer. She hated spying on people, but if there was a murdered walking around, she needed to know. Not only for her own safety, but for the safety of the guests of the bed-and-breakfast and her two new housemates.

"It sounds like we've done all we can, and things are being handled back at the house. Our meeting with Penelope and the detective went longer than expected. Why don't we get something to eat, and then I'll head back," Lizzie suggested as her stomach rumbled, and she realized how late it was.

"I was just going to suggest the same thing. A real meal or quick pizza?"

"A proper meal. Pizza sounds like something I think I'm going to be eating a lot of with teenagers at the house."

Kevin got to his feet and held the chair for Lizzie, snickering as he did.

"Better not let Emma hear you calling her a teenager. We both need to remember she's grown up now. She's no longer Megan's little girl."

"True, where did all the years go? They just seem to run together. Both of us trying to make our careers succeed—"

"You're right, and that's why it's time for us to think about ourselves. Take a little time for ourselves, take the time we should have years ago." Kevin's words could've just been platitudes if Lizzie hadn't looked into his eyes and seen a deeper meaning. They had put their personal relationship on hold for so long she'd given up hope it would ever develop into anything, but in that instant, she saw a spark of something, an unspoken promise.

"I think you're right, Kevin, it's time for us..."

Kevin didn't answer. Instead, he gave her a meaningful smile and held his arm out for her to take. Locking the office behind them, they headed to one of the nicer restaurants just down the street. There is no time like the present to spend some personal time together away from the office, away from college and away from the plantation. It was time for just the two of them to see where things were going to go.

"I CAN'T EAT ANOTHER bite. I haven't eaten this much food in ages. Nora's food is excellent, but this was sublime, and all my favorite foods. I could get used to this."

"It was good, but I don't think I'd want to do it too often. My pants will need to be replaced in a week if we keep this kind of intake up." Kevin patted his stomach for emphasis and put his fork down on the plate to show to the servers they were finished.

Their meal had been a time to catch up, and for over an hour they had talked about just the two of them, the thoughts and dreams for the next stage of their life. Lizzie was done with the college, except for doing consultations, and she looked forward to having free time to discover what her interests might develop into. Kevin had been waiting patiently since their college years for her to come full circle and be his constant companion. But this time, she would not push her feelings aside. This was her time in life, and she was going to enjoy it to the fullest. And this included rekindling her feelings for Kevin.

"I suppose we put it off long enough. I need to head back to the plantation and see what's going on."

"At least we have been occupied enough that the beds should be set up and things should have calmed down by now. Do you want me to come with you?"

"Thanks, Kevin, but I don't think you're up to a house full of women. Not only do I have the two new roommates, Emma and Kelly, but we've got the old college roommates together again, too. And you know what Trish, Piper, and I are like when we get together."

"You're right. I guess I should count it as a blessing that Megan's not here, or you'd have no time for me at all." They shared a smile, but Lizzie didn't bother to deny his accusation. When she and her college roommates got together, they were in their own little world, one that Kevin had always been on the outside of.

They walked down the block to where Lizzie had parked in silence. When they reached the car, she turned to Kevin.

"You'll be out first thing in the morning for the shoot to continue, right?"

Kevin started to answer Lizzie's question, but he was cut off by the ringing of his phone. Holding his finger up to signal for and Lizzie to wait a minute, he quickly answered, and she could hear the deep voice of Detective Mendoza coming through the phone's speakers. The words were unclear, but the tone was somber.

Kevin said little, just a yes, no, and I understand, before he hung up the phone. The look on his face told Lizzie how serious the call had been.

"What's wrong?" Lizzie put her hand on Kevin's arm, and he looked at her slender fingers before he looked into her eyes.

"That was Richard Mendoza. They just found the body of Earl Chambers down by the marketplace."

Lizzie looked around frantically, as if she was expecting the killer to be behind them. Then she shuddered and opened the door of her car.

"I need to get home. I want the others to find out from me, not from the evening news."

"Hang on, and I'll come with you."

"No, Kevin, the detective trusts you. Use that to your advantage. Go down to the murder scene and find out as much as you can."

Lizzie didn't wait to see if Kevin was going to agree with her. She hopped in the car and turned the engine on and moments later was heading back to Azalea Plantation.

Chapter 25

Lizzie stood on the front steps of her home and wondered if it would ever be peaceful again. She had planned on slowly moving the furniture in, piece by piece, to make sure everything was perfect. But of course, plans never go the way you expect them too, and instead, she had to step out of the way of two guys carrying a box spring through the front door and up the stairs.

She followed behind him and stood looking around. This was not the orderly home she was used to. Backpacks were set by the front door, they'd tossed two navy blue sweatshirts over the railing to the stairs, and music was blaring from the kitchen. Somebody had brought a radio and turned it on, and as the others worked, they were shouting over the music.

"Hey, Lizzie, we're all upstairs. Come on up and see what we've done."

Trisha's voice reached Lizzie, and she looked up to see Trisha and Piper leaning over the railing of the mezzanine, waving. Swallowing a gulp, Lizzie pasted on a smile and returned their wave.

"Coming through, watch yourself."

Josh's voice sounded from behind Lizzie, and she turned to see him and one student from the college carrying the mattress belonging to the box spring that had gone up before them.

"Sorry, I'll get out of the way." Lizzie only stepped away from the staircase and watched the muscular arms of the men lift the mattress easily, as if it weighed no more than a box of paper towels, and head upstairs.

"I'd better check out what's going on up there," Lizzie mumbled to herself, and followed the two men.

When she reached the mezzanine, she found things weren't as chaotic as she thought they would be. Nora Meadows was in charge, which meant things would go smoothly. She was directing the men where to put the mattresses, although it was hard not to see the frames on the floor waiting. In her arms, she had bedding ready to make up the beds.

"Well, I bet you didn't think you're going to have a guest quite this quickly, did you?" The older woman grinned at Lizzie, and she seemed pleased with the way things were going.

"Things never seem to go the way you plan, do they?" Lizzie answered with a wry grin.

"No need to fret. We'll have these beds set up in no time. The guys are bringing up yours next. Then tomorrow, we can work on the rest of the furniture, but at least tonight you'll all have a comfortable spot to sleep in." Nora shifted the bedding enough that she could reach out and pat Lizzie on the shoulder.

The clumping of footsteps on the stairs announced Kelly and Emma. Both girls were eager to share with Lizzie their harrowing incident of earlier. Lizzie listened calmly, having heard most of it from Trisha, letting the girls get it all out of their system.

"I know some people think I left the light on in that cabin by myself and just forgot about it, but I didn't. I really appreciate you letting me stay here with you and Kelly," Emma finished with a huff glaring at Trisha who must've doubted whether she had seen the light.

"Well, maybe it's best you're here, anyway; you can keep Kelly company. It's better not to take any chances, especially with the murderer still on the loose," Trisha added, her way of apologizing for doubting the younger girl.

"I really can stay here?" Kelly asked, looking around at the others as if she expected them to renege on the offer.

"For as long as you need to, Kelly. We spoke with social services, and they'll be out tomorrow morning to talk with you and make sure you're going to be okay here, but I think we can make it work." Lizzie reassured her with a smile.

By this time, Piper and Trisha had joined them, and Trisha turned her attention to Kelly.

"All I can say is you must be pretty special. In all the years that I've been here on the plantation, both in my youth and as an adult, the Higgins ghost has never appeared in front of me."

"So, you believe me? You really believe there's a ghost here?" The four women laughed, and Nora called from across the room, "There's more than one ghost here. Elizabeth Higgins's old housekeeper shows up every once in a while.

But like you, Kelly, I've never seen Elizabeth Higgins's ghost either, just the housekeeper."

Not wanting to get all caught up in talk of ghosts and ghostly visits, Lizzie motioned for quiet and then made her announcement about Earl.

"Kelly, I'm sorry. I don't know how well you knew Earl, but they discovered his body in town today." There was a collective gasp from those in the room, and Kelly took a step backward, as if she was ready to run.

"There's nothing to worry about, and the police are going to have additional patrols around the plantation, and Kevin is going to hire more security. I just want you to be aware of what's going on and look out for each other. That goes for everybody, Trisha. Nobody wanders off on their own, whether crew or residents of the plantation." Lizzie turned from looking at Trisha and Kelly and focused her attention on her housekeeper. "We'll put a warning up for the guests over at the bed-and-breakfast, Nora. I don't think it'll be a problem, but they have a right to know what's going on."

"I'll get right on that. What a shame. He seemed like a nice man. A little lost and without purpose, but harmless." Lizzie looked at the housekeeper who grinned, surprised she wasn't aware Nora had spent any time with Earl. Seeing her expression, Nora explained.

"He wandered into my kitchen several times in between running errands for that Camille. Like I said, he was pleasant and more than helpful, but way too hung up on a woman who couldn't spare him a pleasant word."

Lizzie nodded. That fit in with what she had heard as well. Which made her wonder why anybody would want to murder the quiet man. Did he know something, something about Camille or her murder? Before they could say anything more, the men were back with another box springs and mattress. It was getting crowded in the room, and Nora took charge again.

"All right, girls, head over to the bed-and-breakfast. The chef's got a meal waiting for you, and we need to be out of the men's way so they can get their work done and eat as well."

Dropping the bedding on the first bed that was already set up, Nora waved her arms like an old farmer's wife waving the chickens out to feed. A few moments later, with Harry leading the way, Emma and Kelly, followed by Piper, Trisha, and Lizzie, were walking across the lawn toward the plantation house. In no time, Lizzies friends were sitting down at a table, their plates filled with delicious-smelling pasta, talking about the plans for the next day. Lizzie took a seat and placed a tall glass of iced tea in front of her, she was stuffed from her meal with Kevin, but wanted to join in with the others. As they ate, Lizzie noticed Nora was leading the way with Josh and his helpers toward the back door of the kitchen. They'd worked up an appetite, and she was going to make sure everybody got their fill.

They kept the talk of murder away from the dining room guests, and instead, Lizzie, Piper, and Trisha regaled those at the table with stories of their college antics. Lizzie shared a knowing glance with her two friends. There would be enough talk of murder tomorrow.

Chapter 26

The branches of the live oak outside Lizzie's window knocked against the glass panes in the morning breeze, bringing a mixture of urgency and anticipation.

Lizzie lay in bed for a moment, Harry's not so gentle snoring coming from the pillow above her head. She reached her arm above her head and stroked the cat, giving him an extra scratch under the chin.

"Harry, a gentleman doesn't snore."

But the cat didn't even open his eyes, and experience had taught her Harry would get up when he was ready and not until. She heard a sound from the room across the hall and remembered that she had house guests. She'd been sleeping on the blow-up bed for the last couple of nights and had to admit the firm mattress and the soft pillows made a welcome difference. Getting herself out of bed, she was quiet, not wanting to wake the rest of the household. Piper had a room over at the bed-and-breakfast, and it had been late when Trisha had headed for her own home the night before.

As Lizzie washed her face and brushed her teeth, she went over in her mind what was on the morning agenda.

"Penelope will be here around nine, and I somehow have to get ahold of Detective Mendoza and find out what happened to Earl," she told herself as she brushed her hair. Looking in the mirror, she snapped her fingers. "Or maybe I won't. I have heard nothing new from Kevin. Let's hope he got the information from his friend."

Harry rubbed against her ankles at the sound of her voice, reminding her he hadn't had breakfast and he wanted to be sure she didn't forget about feeding him.

In no time, Lizzie was dressed and padding down the staircase, Harry close behind. She made sure the girls were still sleeping and closed their door firmly so they would not be woken by her activities downstairs. There was still time before Penelope would show up, or the rest of the film crew. She'd let them enjoy a few moments of extra sleep.

The first thing she needed to do was to meet Harry's needs, and she swiftly put his breakfast down on the floor mat with his name on it, and then started making coffee.

Yeah, this is all I need, a coffee maker and microwave. I'll send the girls over to the plantation house for breakfast, which means my kitchen stays clean, and I don't have to use any of those appliances Nora insisted I have, she thought to herself smugly.

Once her coffee was finished, she poured a cup and walked out to sit on the front porch and watch the plantation come to life. The swans were gracefully swimming in the pond, oblivious to the excitement that had happened there recently. It didn't seem to bother them. Harry meandered out and sat next to her until he heard a squirrel in the nearby tree. Jumping up on the railing, he paced to see where the animal was.

"Never mind, Harry, you're too fat for chasing squirrels. It would be just your luck that you would jump up the tree to race after him and get stuck. Then you'd be embarrassed if I had to call the fire department to get you down."

Harry looked at her and growled with a snap of his tail. He did not try to chase the chattering squirrel above him, and Lizzie wondered if the growl was for her or the squirrel.

Turning her gaze toward the bed-and-breakfast, Lizzie watched the door of the kitchen open and saw Josh walking toward the greenhouse, clipboard in hand. She shook her head, wondering how he could write and walk at the same time. But he did, and even more irritating was the fact that his penmanship was so good, and she could easily read what he wrote. Lizzie knew he was deep into the final stages of getting a patent on a new breed of roses, and that was occupying his mind more than anything else.

As she watched, more activity gave evidence that the guests at the bed-and-breakfast were waking up and getting ready to explore the garden. That was one attraction for guests. Lizzie was always amazed at how diehard some of her guests were. Some even arranging their vacation so they could take part in different workshops that Josh and his crew held at the greenhouse. Even the children enjoyed it, and they had a special children's garden set up with smaller tools that small hands could handle.

Harry was not that happy about the children's garden. Because that meant there was always somebody small closer to the ground who could easily reach out and grab his tail. Lizzie wasn't sure what he disliked more; having his tail pulled or hearing the high-pitched squeals of delight when the children saw him.

"Looks like the day is coming to life, Harry."

Lizzie took another sip of her coffee and watched two vans head toward the back garden. The film crew was here, and she sent a quick text to Piper, letting her know they had arrived. She received the acknowledgment from Piper, just as Trisha arrived kicking up dust along the dirt road.

"Come on, Harry, we need to make sure the girls are up and ready to get to work."

Opening the door, she walked in to hear the sounds of the kitchen cupboard doors being opened and closed. She followed the sound and saw two sleepy-looking girls staring at the coffeepot.

"You have to pour it before you can drink it, Emma."

"Yeah, but that takes energy. I am not a morning person. But you look like you are. How long have you been up?"

"Long enough to get my first cup of coffee in. How did you sleep, Kelly?"

Lizzie walked over and picked up the coffeepot as she answered. Without being asked, she poured a cup of coffee for each of the girls and took the third chair at the kitchen counter.

"Wonderfully. Thank you. I heard the crew arriving. I guess we better get moving." Kelly took a deep breath of the powerful aroma of coffee as she answered. Emma wasn't so patient. She hurriedly sipped the coffee and sighed as the first taste of the strong liquid hit her taste buds.

"If you two want breakfast, you have to go over to the main house."

"No, coffee is good enough for me. I'm ready to get to work," Emma answered, and Kelly nodded in agreement.

"Finish your coffee and then head out. But I want the two of you to stick together. And Kelly, the woman from social services will be here a little later this morning, and she's going to want to talk to you."

Kelly sighed as if she had the weight of the world on her shoulders. But Emma gave Kelly a nudge in the ribs with her elbow and gave her an encouraging smile.

"Hang in there, Kelly. We've got your back. Things always work out the way they're supposed to, so just have faith. After all, you're staying in this fantastic place, ghosts and all."

Lizzie and Kelly laughed with Emma, and the mood lightened considerably. Both girls finished their coffee in no time and headed out the kitchen screen door to join the other film crew members. As they walked out, Piper and Trisha walked in.

"Can you two help organize the equipment? We'll be out in a moment." Trisha said, as she passed the two girls.

"Good morning," Lizzie greeted her two friends, "are we continuing to film what we started yesterday?"

"Yes, and we want to get some additional shots before we're ready for you to come in and do your introduction segment." Trisha answered. She walked across the kitchen and helped herself to a cup of coffee. Old habits die hard, and she automatically poured one for Piper, and then topped off Lizzie's cup, just as if they were still living together off campus.

"Any more news on Earl?" Settling into the chair Emma had just abandoned, Trisha looked at Lizzie with concern.

"I talked with Kevin last night just briefly, and he confirmed that yes, it was a murder. He'll be out here in an hour, and I'll get more information. But just like I told the two girls that just walked out the door, be on the lookout and take care of each other. Someone out there is a murderer. And I think it's somebody involved in the film crew."

"Two murders? And you think they are both connected?" Piper interjected.

"How can they not be?"

"Do you think it has anything to do with who was searching Emma's cabin?" Piper asked, concern clear in her voice.

Lizzie and Trisha exchanged a look, and then Lizzie gave a shrug.

"I doubt it. Somebody was just being nosy. Somebody who has no business being here." Lizzie pressed her lips firmly closed and said nothing else. She had an idea who it might've been, but she wouldn't accuse anybody without evidence. Taking her cue, the other two dropped the subject and finished the coffee. Moments later, they were out the door, and Lizzie could hear Trisha welcoming the crew back and Piper giving instructions.

"I hope Kevin gets here before Penelope. I want to see if he found out anything else." Harry jumped up on the counter and bumped heads with Lizzie as she murmured to herself.

Chapter 27

Lizzie was just putting the last cup on the drain rack to dry when she heard Kevin's voice from the front door calling out a good morning. A few moments later, he wandered into the kitchen carrying a plate covered with a linen napkin.

"I come bearing gifts. The chef noticed nobody had come over for breakfast, so he sent some Danishes to tide you all over. And a message from Nora to make sure nobody skips lunch."

Lizzie grinned as she lifted the corner of the napkin and saw her favorite Danish sitting there tempting her. With a sigh, she gave into the temptation and grabbed one off the plate. She would never maintain her weight at a healthy level if she kept eating like this. Kevin put the plate down on the counter and grabbed one for himself, and in unison, they let out a contented sigh.

"This is so much better than the burnt toast I had at my house," Kevin made a face before taking another bite, and Lizzie laughed at his expression.

"Oh, come on, Kevin, even I can make toast without burning it."

"Yeah, well, I was preoccupied. I was on the phone with Richard." Lizzie's head snapped up, and she stared at him. She knew of only one Richard, and that was the detective. If he had called Kevin that early in the morning, there must've been a fresh development. With one hand on her hip and the other hand still holding the Danish, she waited for his explanation.

"They determined Earl was definitely murdered. And there's a positive connection to Camille's murder."

"I knew it!"

"Apparently, Camille's missing phone was in Earl's pocket."

"I hope they won't try to pin Camille's murder on Earl. It just makes little sense."

"The detective agrees with that. The man adored her and had no reason to kill her. But the question is, how did he end up with her phone? And there's more; Richard is asking for your help." Even as he spoke, Kevin was pulling his own phone out of his pocket and making a few swipes across the screen as he brought up what he wanted Lizzie to look at.

"Richard sent this to me. I think he is stumped. Camille made cryptic notes about her employees, and he'd like you to figure out what they mean."

Lizzie held her hand out for the phone, but Kevin hesitated as if he was having second thoughts.

"A few casual questions and some simple eavesdropping should be all it takes to get him the information. You don't need to be any more involved than that, Lizzie."

"You worry too much, Kevin. I have no intention of putting myself or those around me in danger. I've already been through that once. I don't want to go through it again."

"I always knew you were smart; good to see you can still learn lessons from your actions." Kevin said, as Lizzie took the phone from his hand.

"Don't be snarky," she scolded him absentmindedly as she read the screen from the phone. There were several notations, but only four of them concerned her, a simple phrase about each of the four crew members.

Kelly—on the run

Tony—not who you think you are

Ophelia—money for nothing

Tiffany—the great pretender

"Well, those are cryptic. They remind me of song lyrics. What was she thinking?" Lizzie took another bite of her Danish and stared at the screen as if waiting for an answer to pop up.

But before Kevin could answer, her front doorbell rang, and Lizzie glanced over at the clock, surprised to see how much time had passed.

"That will be the woman from social services. Stay here, Kevin, maybe your presence will convince her that this is a stable place for Kelly." Lizzie shot him a pleading look as she headed to the front door.

"I'M SURE THIS WILL work out just fine for Kelly. Having stability, even for a short time, will do her a world of good. I can't thank you enough for opening your home to her, Professor Higgins."

Penelope held her hand out to shake with Lizzie with a warm smile. With the other hand, she was opening the door, ready to head over to the dining room to grab a cup of coffee and brunch. Lizzie knew full well she was also going to be checking out plantation facilities, but she had no worries. Nora would give Penelope a guided tour and help reassure the woman that Kelly would be safe here. Lizzie knew once she met the staff running the vacation spot, any last fear or unease she might have would be settled.

"Thank you, Penelope. And like I said, Kelly has a place here as long as she needs it, and we'll make sure she stays safe and out of trouble."

The older woman laughed, her short, curly head bobbing with amusement. Her plump cheeks were flushed with pleasure. It was obvious she was pleased with the outcome of her visit.

"We'll do the best we can between the two of us, Professor Higgins. But don't forget she's a teenager; and trouble and teenagers go together. Our primary focus is safety. I am confident it won't be an issue as long as she stays here under your supervision."

And with that, Penelope pushed the door open, nodded her head at Kevin, who stood behind Lizzie, and headed over to talk with Nora Meadows.

"Well, looks like you've got a houseguest for an indefinite period of time," Kevin said as they watched Penelope walk across the lawn. He'd been silent for most of Penelope's visit, asking a few questions and answering when spoken to, but this was Lizzie's deal, and he was more than willing to let her step up and take control. He just hoped she wouldn't regret the decision to suddenly have somebody living with her when she had been looking so forward to solitude and having a place to herself.

"You know, I think she'll fit right in. And at least we know the resident ghost approves of her. After all, Elizabeth is the one who led the two girls to my door."

"So she says. I don't know whether to be jealous or relieved that Kelly is the only one other than you alive who has ever seen Elizabeth Higgins. In all the years we've known each other, she's never shown herself to me."

"It is odd, isn't it? Oh, did you know there's another resident ghost? Apparently, Nora's been seeing it for years."

"Okay, now you're just messing with me. There's no way Nora would agree there's a ghost wandering the plantation."

"Oh, she swears there is. Apparently, the ghost is an old housekeeper who's not above playing pranks on individuals that she doesn't think deserve to stay at the plantation. Right now, it seems like Freddie is the one who is subject to her pranks."

With a laugh, Lizzie told Kevin about the episode in the kitchen. As she spoke, she remembered all those times that Freddie had complained about somebody tripping him by holding the door closed and, with a smirk, she realized it was probably the ghostly housekeeper.

"You know, I can't think of anybody else who deserves to be haunted by ghosts than Freddie." Kevin's shoulders shook with laughter. Then he turned serious.

"So, what do you think of that message I sent you earlier? Do any of Camille's notes make sense to you?"

Lizzie turned serious as she thought about Kevin's question.

"My first reaction is that she's writing in code, and she's noting specific facts about each of those people. Kelly is obvious. We all know she's a runaway. And we know Camille held that over her head to make sure that Kelly would work for her at a lower rate and not question what she was told to do."

"There were quite a few people she had listed—"

"You're right. I think we need to concentrate on those who are involved with the filming here at the plantation. Ophelia, Tiffany, and Tony seem to be our prime suspects. We need to find out what Camille had on them and how far they would go to keep what she knew a secret."

"And how do you plan on doing that?"

"I don't think it'll take more than a few pointed questions. Now that the threat Camille had over them as a unit is gone, I have a feeling it would not take much for them to turn on each other. And I'm pretty sure they know each other's secrets."

Lizzie and Kevin looked at each other for a moment, and then before Kevin could warn her off, Lizzie added, "A discrete few questions, Kevin. I promise I won't put anybody in the line of fire, including myself. Does that make you feel better?"

"Not really. But I have little choice but to accept it. Somehow, you always seem to go above and beyond what you say you're going to do, and I just hope it doesn't land you in trouble."

Chapter 28

Kevin gave a slow nod of agreement and stretched his hand out to the plate as if to grab another Danish. But before he could reach it, Lizzie leaned over and pulled the plate out of his reach. As she did, a necklace she was wearing came free from the folds of her shirt. Kevin adjusted the movement of his hand and instead reached over and touched the key on the end of the chain.

"How long have you been wearing this?"

"Since the first night that I moved into the house. I don't know why; it just seemed appropriate. I mean, you and I found it hidden in the outside fireplace, walled up in the stone. There was a reason Elizabeth Higgins took such care to hide the key, and now that I've moved in here, I feel like I'm responsible for it, like I am its keeper."

"You don't mean possessive, like a Hobbit type of keeper?" Kevin smiled, but there was concern in his voice as well.

"Don't be silly," Lizzie scoffed. "It's just a sense of responsibility, family responsibility, to be honest. I don't know what this key opens or what I'll find inside, but it was special to my ancestor, and when I find it, I want to be ready to open whatever it is."

"No other reason?"

"Freddie is making me nervous, to be honest. He's over here a lot more than he has been in the past. Says he wants to watch the construction, but he never seems to be in the construction zone. He's always scurrying around looking at other things. I just don't want him to get his hands on something he shouldn't."

"You don't think he will try anything, do you?"

"Oh, I don't worry about Freddie. Physically, he'd never get his hands dirty, or his clothes soiled. But if there was an underhanded way to get what he wants, he'll use it. I know one thing; he will not be happy about the extra security that was added to the house yesterday while we were in town."

Kevin gave her a swift look to reassure himself that she wasn't worried about Freddie. He had to agree Freddie was no threat physically, but he was sneaky, and in a Snidely Whiplash type of way. Without even thinking about it, Kevin raised his hands to his mouth and made the motion of curling a mustache. Lizzie watched his motion and burst out laughing.

"Exactly what I'm thinking," she said.

Dropping the necklace, Kevin gave one more longing glance at the plate of Danishes, and then asked Lizzie what her first step would be.

"I think I'm going to get them to turn against each other or at least tell each other's secrets. And it's important they don't know that Camille's phone was found. I have a feeling if they believe they are above suspicion, they'll work hard to make somebody else seem like a more likely target."

"That might work if you don't push too hard. Just be careful not to let anybody get their defenses up so much that they feel like they're backed into a corner. Then flight or fight syndrome will take place, and you'll either get no further information, or you'll put yourself in danger." As he spoke, Kevin reached out and grabbed Lizzie's hand, squeezing it in warning.

"I'm just fishing Kevin; I promise I'll back off if I feel I'm pushing too hard." Lizzie squeezed his hand back to reassure him.

"There's no time like the present to get started. It looks like they're all separated on different tasks. I'm going to start with Ophelia. She's the most nervous and the most likely to spill the beans about somebody else."

"What do you need me to do?"

"Can you wander around the site? You keep an eye out on Emma and Kelly. I don't want them in danger or trying to run their own investigation. Emma's too much like her mother, and if she gets an idea, she'll go with it without thinking about the results."

Kevin quickly agreed with her assessment, and the two of them walked to the back door. He held it open for her, and when they reached the bottom of the stairs, they each went in an opposite direction. Kevin headed toward Piper and Trisha, who were giving directions to Tony. Lizzie, with Harry following closely behind, moved toward Ophelia.

Ophelia was standing away from the others, busy with the clipboard she had in her hand, checking off items. She didn't notice Lizzie walking toward her until Lizzie was almost in front of her.

"Good morning, Ophelia," Lizzie said in a soft voice to make sure she didn't startle the woman. Ophelia looked up and smiled brightly at Lizzie, returning the greeting. Lizzie couldn't help noticing how at ease the woman looked. The tension seemed to be gone from her tight shoulders, and her smile was genuine, not the forced smile Lizzie had seen when working around Camille.

"How's everything going this morning? You need help with anything?" Lizzie asked, wanting to be sure the woman felt at ease and not singled out.

"No, I think I've got everything under control. I'm just going over these last-minute changes that Piper gave me this morning. She's wonderful to work with, quite the visionary. She made a few changes to the angles that we'll be filming, and I think it'll work much better. Yesterday we were fighting with the glare of the sun through the trees."

"It helps that she's got the photographer's mind. She can look through a lens and see things that the rest of us don't. You'll want to see her gallery. Some photos that she has put on display are just outstanding."

"That's definitely on my list of things to do." Ophelia gave a nod and agreed.

"Well, I really wanted to just check and make sure you're not uncomfortable working here. I mean, with the murder..."

"I should be, but I'm not. I actually feel like a weight's been lifting off my shoulder. Not having Camille around here makes the job, well, pleasant. She was a brilliant woman, but she just had no people skills, and she was manipulative. Just look at the way she treated poor Earl. Getting him to do all kinds of odd jobs, never paying him, just so he could be her groupie. That's not right."

"Who knows what caused her murderer to snap."

Ophelia's head jerked up, and she looked at Lizzie directly.

"I know the police questioned us, but they can't possibly think it was one of us who killed her. It wouldn't make sense. I mean, I know Camille was hard on people, and she definitely hinted that she knew things about each of us, but that was just a power play."

"Do you really think so, Ophelia? I seem to think it might be otherwise. I mean, Emma was telling us about the way she treated Kelly, holding Kelly's secret over her head—"

"You mean the secret that Kelly was a runaway? It was no secret; we all knew it. But you're right. She held it over Kelly's head. Maybe Kelly was the one who snapped. Fear can do crazy things to people, that's for sure."

Ophelia clipped her pen to the clipboard, and before Lizzie could ask questions, she excused herself and scurried away like the mouse she had been called in Kelly's notebook. Lizzie watched her progress and found she didn't feel so warm toward the woman. It irritated her how quick she'd been to throw Kelly under the bus, and that raised more suspicion than it answered questions.

Chapter 29

Emma and Kelly were occupied with moving accessories around the terrace to begin the day's filming. Piper had specifically asked for a few pieces to be brought over from the plantation to make the patio feel more lived in.

"Look, Lizzie's in sleuth mode." Emma gave Kelly a nudge to her ribs and used her head to nod in Lizzie's direction. Kelly turned her attention to where Lizzie was talking to Ophelia.

"It looks like she knows what she's doing. Ophelia doesn't look like she's ready to run away." Kelly watched the interaction between the two women before she spoke.

"Well, other than the fact that Lizzie has a natural way of talking to people, and yes, she has investigated another murder before. So have Piper and my mom."

"Really? That means you're going to be a natural crime solver, aren't you?"

"Not me. There's no way I want to put myself in a dangerous situation. It might be all fun and exciting to figure out who killed somebody, but it's also dangerous. And I've got too much ahead of me to take a foolish chance like that. Besides, I don't think I'm as inquisitive as the other women." Emma gave a bark of laughter as she shook her head in disagreement.

The two girls got back to work, but Emma's attention was soon diverted by somebody walking around the vans parked where they were yesterday. She stopped what she was doing and squinted her eyes, trying to get a better look. But the person she was watching had his back to her and was moving in a way that appeared to be a deliberate attempt to keep from being seen. Emma watched as he disappeared behind the vans and waited, but he didn't reappear. Giving a last glance toward Lizzie and Trish, she turned her attention back to what she was doing.

"Come on Emma, it'll only take one more trip to bring the stuff over from the plantation, and then we're done." Kelly straightened her back, using her hands on her hips for balance, stretching backwards to work out the kinks from hauling the lounge chair.

"Right, the sooner we are done, the sooner the crew can start filming. I think today Lizzie is going to do her bit on film as well. She's a natural in front of the camera, and it really shows how much she loves not only the plantation but the gardening. She won't say it out loud, but she's been really excited about the renovation of this old house and bringing the gardens back to life." Emma nodded and mimicked Kelly's motion to release the strain on her back.

"I've picked up on that over the last couple days, even with all the other stuff going on. Emma, you believe I saw that woman leading us to the house, don't you?"

Emma studied Kelly for a moment before she answered. "Yes. And I know who you saw, but she had your best interest in mind. And I know Lizzie has seen her as well."

"But you didn't see her?"

"I saw something, but I can't say with certainty what it was. And it doesn't matter. I believe you; that's what matters."

Emma watched her friend visibly relax, and a smile broke over her face. "Thanks. I was doubting myself. Come on, let's get that last piece we need for here."

Throwing her arm over Kelly's shoulder, Emma led the way across the lawn toward the main house. As they rounded the pond, Emma couldn't help but look across to where they had found the body and was surprised to see somebody standing on the pier next to the swan boat. There was something familiar about him, and she called out a morning greeting.

The man she was calling out to seemed startled and almost fell into the water before he turned, looked at Emma and Kelly, and then scurried back down the pier to the boathouse, disappearing from view. In an instant, Emma realized it was the same person she had seen over by the vans. And this time, she had recognized him.

"I wonder what Lizzie's cousin Freddie is up to now. There's something about that man that I just don't like."

"I don't think you're the only one. He reminds me of a weasel always sneaking around, giving you the feeling he'd turn on you in a second." Kelly had also watched the man scurry away.

The girls continued to the plantation house, and thoughts of Freddie disappeared when Nora opened the door to greet them with a picnic basket in one hand and coffee in the other.

"Perfect timing. I was just getting ready to walk across to give the crew some morning sustenance. I'll wait and walk across with you two," Nora said.

The girls agreed and hurriedly gathered the last items from the list Piper had given them. Ten minutes later, the three were on the patio, spreading out their wares. While Emma added the pillows to the lounge chair where Lizzie would sit to talk to the camera, Kelly helped Nora place the food from the picnic basket and the coffee on the table they had set up the day before. It was as if the aroma of the coffee called to the workers, and in no time, everybody was gathered by the table, taking a quick break. Even Freddie showed up, this time not trying to hide his presence.

Emma watched Lizzie greet her cousin politely but not overly warmly. Trisha pointedly ignored him. She'd learned her lesson years ago about encouraging Freddie into conversation. As Emma watched Freddie, he reached into his pocket and pulled out a monogrammed hanky to daintily wiped the corners of his mouth where the Danish had smeared its sugary substance. Emma's eyes grew wide in surprise, and she grabbed Kelly's hand and dragged her friend over to stand next to Freddie.

"You were the one searching my cabin. Why?" Emma didn't bother with pleasant greetings. Instead, she glared at Freddy, her hands on her hips, her voice low so that the others wouldn't hear her.

"I don't know what you're talking about. Go away." Freddie hissed back and made a shooing motion with his hands.

But Emma stood her ground and casually reached into her pocket and pulled out a matching white linen hanky that she had stuffed into her pocket on a whim when she got dressed this morning, hoping to find out who it belonged to.

"I think this belongs to you, Freddie. You dropped it by the bed in my cabin. You can't deny it. It perfectly matches the one in your hand."

"Mind your own business, and don't worry about what I'm doing. I have just as much right to be in those cabins as anybody else. I was just checking to make sure you weren't destroying it with your lifestyle." Freddie snatched the hanky from her hand, sneering.

Emma was furious, and she took a step closer to Freddie, snatching the hanky back.

"Watch yourself, Freddie. I don't think Lizzie would want to know you're snooping around so much. I don't know what you're up to, but you'd better think about your actions before somebody catches you snooping around and gets physical with you."

Freddie glared at Emma, his mouth open like a fish on land, gasping for air.

"Are you threatening me?" he finally managed to ask.

"Try anything else, and you'll find out."

Before Freddie or Emma could continue their conversation, another car pulled up, and everybody's attention turned to watch Kate walk across to join them. When Emma turned back to say something more to Freddie, she found he had scurried away while everybody's attention was diverted.

"You're right, Kelly. He is a weasel." Kelly exchanged a knowing look with Emma and then turned her attention back to Kate's arrival.

Chapter 30

Lizzie watched Kate meander across the lawn to join them. She greeted everybody with a friendly smile, but for once, she didn't cozy up with Kevin. Lizzie raised her eyebrows in surprise. Usually, Kate would have her arm linked with Kevin's by now and would be flirting outrageously, but this morning, she was treating him the same as everyone else. Lizzie couldn't help but feel a sense of relief. She hadn't realized how much it bothered her to watch Kate interact with Kevin.

The new arrival helped herself to a cup of coffee Nora offered and then asked intelligent questions about the setup for filming that they were planning. After a few moments, Piper clapped her hands together and ordered everybody to get back to work, leaving Lizzie, Kevin, Trisha, and Kate standing next to each other. Nora was busy cleaning up the break area, not paying any attention to them.

"Can we go inside? I have some information I don't think you want anybody else to overhear," Kate asked Lizzie, who quickly nodded in agreement and led the way to her downstairs office. Lizzie was the last to enter, closing the door behind her, turning her attention to Kate.

"What's up, Kate?" she asked bluntly.

For once Kate didn't seem her normally competent self and twisted a strand of hair as she looked at the others watching her.

"Okay, this doesn't go any farther than this room, but I'm admitting defeat. I am stumped on finding out information about Camille's employees. Kelly is the only one I could find out who she was and what her problems were. And that was only because I was able to find some gossips from the homes she was in, not from official records. Ophelia had some problems at her job and left, but when I tried to talk to her past employers, they clammed up and wouldn't say a word to me."

"Not a word? Are you losing your powers, Kate?" Trisha laughed.

That seemed to be the goading Kate needed, and she stiffened her back and glared at Trisha. "Not on your life. I'm stumped, but I'm not out. It could take me a little longer to find the information, but I wanted to let you know what I have found, so maybe you can work things from your end. Kevin, maybe you can get the detective to open up some files I don't have access to, especially on Tony."

Kevin gave a nod and waited in anticipation, wondering what she would have to say about Tony.

"The only thing I could find out about him that's proof positive is that Tony is not his real name. But I can't find out any more than that. My first reaction was that he was in witness protection." Kate paused and placed her hands on her hips, almost in defiance, as she looked back at the three watching her. "Oh, come on. You guys have been around him even more than me—his mouth never shuts up. If he was in witness protection, he would've blurted it out to somebody by now."

The others agreed, and Lizzie gave Kate an inquiring look.

"I wasn't aware you were so familiar with Tony. Are you holding out on us?"

"I saw him at the bar in town and tried to cozy up to him and get information when he first came to town. I was trying to figure out a line for a story on the production out here. He was all too willing to talk about himself but didn't give me any other information, and as I started checking what he told me, it was all packed with lies." Kate gave an unladylike snort before she continued. "Besides, there's no way I'd be interest in Tony when I've started seeing someone else."

Lizzie could feel the smile tug at the corner of her mouth, and she raised her hand to rub her nose and hide her expression.

So that's why there's none of the usual flirting with Kevin.

Glancing over at Kevin, she saw him visibly relax his shoulders, and she dropped her hand to her side, not bothering to hide her smile. It looks like he was relieved Kate would no longer be pursuing him as well.

Lizzie turned her attention back to Kate to hear what the woman had to say next when she caught the glimpse of something outside the window. Casually moving in that direction, she looked out the window, only to find nothing there. It must've been a trick of the light, she thought to herself.

"Kelly Sky we know about. I can't tell you what a relief it is to know that she's going to be safe here at Azalea Plantation. Runaways get lost in the system so often, and she is a bright girl. I think with some guidance and support she could really go places." Kate grinned her approval at Lizzie, but shook her head when Lizzie asked how Kate had found out about Kelly. The reporter was going to keep her sources to herself.

"I agree, and she is a very bright girl. I've already told her caseworker she can stay as long as she needs to while the case is being solved. But I don't think I'm going to stick to that timeline. I'd like to help her out as much as I can, and I'm going to talk to Penelope about making it an open-ended invitation."

Kevin and Trisha nodded. They had each talked to Lizzie about Kelly and expressed their approval of her plan.

"That's great, Lizzie. If there's anything I can do to help, let me know," Kate offered.

There was a sudden sound of something crashing in the hallway, causing everyone to jump and turn toward the door. Kevin was the first to reach it, and when he whipped it open, he was surprised to find a stack of boxes that had been outside the door had been pushed to the side causing several of them to topple over creating the sudden noise. But there was no sign of anyone who might have pushed the pile.

Lizzie peered around him, wondering what was going on. Then she remembered how her attention had been diverted to the window, and without saying a word, she hurried back to the window just in time to see a dark shadow let go of the branch. What surprised her even more was the branch seemed to be targeted at an eavesdropper outside the window.

Lizzie reached out to the crank on the window to open it wider, but her movements had been detected, and her cousin Freddie disappeared around the corner of the house.

"Freddie!" she cried out to the disappearing figure, slapping the windowsill.

"What trouble is he up to now?" asked Trish as she joined Lizzie.

"And just how much did he hear of our conversation?" Lizzie murmured under her breath.

"It's a good thing there was a commotion in the hallway to stop us from saying anything else," Trisha replied with a knowing look.

Lizzie looked at her friend and then looked back at the doorway where Kevin and Kate stood looking back at her. She agreed with Trisha's assessment. It was a good thing there had been a commotion to distract their conversation. The timing was perfect, almost as if somebody else had been listening and tried to keep them from saying anything more.

"Everything okay?" Kate asked Lizzie with her reporter curiosity.

"Yes, did you find out anything about Tiffany?" Lizzie answered, turning the conversation back to what they had been talking about.

Kate let out a puff of exasperated air and scratched her head before she answered.

"Again, just the bare minimum. I know what state she was born in. I know what county. But beyond that, she's a mystery. She has no social media presence. She has no ties to anyone from where she came from. It's as if she wanted to disappear from her hometown."

"So, each of them has kept their past hidden," Kevin said.

"And that makes me think Camille had found out something. Something about one or all of them. Something that frightened her murderer enough to take action." Lizzie walked over to stand in front of the chalkboard and picked up a piece of chalk as she spoke. She was tempted to write the suspect's names on the board, but she knew there were enough opportunities for them to wander into the house and be nosy and discover what they were up to. It wasn't worth the chance. With more force than she intended, she slammed the chalk back down on the tray, breaking it.

"Easy Lizzie, you will figure it out." Trisha laughed and gave her a thumbs-up motion with her hand. But Lizzie wasn't so sure. She was positive Earl's murder was tied to Camille, which meant it was tied to the film crew. And that meant there was still a murderer wandering around Azalea Plantation.

Chapter 31

The knock on the door interrupted their conversation, and Lizzie watched as the door opened and Piper stuck her head in.

"I'm really sorry to interrupt you guys, but I need your help here for a moment. I want to try something different, and I want to get some feedback from you. Do you have a second?" Kevin and Trisha immediately nodded and moved toward the door, but Lizzie hesitated, looking at Kate.

"You two go ahead. I'll catch up with everyone in a minute. I just need to ask Kate a couple of questions."

"Sure, take your time. Trisha and Kevin can get me started, and then you can have the final say. We'll be out where the old gazebo is," Piper told Lizzie and then motioned for Kevin and Trisha to follow her.

When they had left the range of hearing, Lizzie turned back to Kate. "You have no other concrete evidence about the three of them?" Lizzie asked, referring to the three suspects.

"I wish I did. I mean, I can tell you that Tiffany is from a small parish in Louisiana, but it's such a mixture of people that it is hard to tell what side of the track she's from." Kate shrugged.

"Well, Tony's going to be easy because he likes to brag, and difficult because he likes to lie." Lizzie tapped her forefinger to her chin as she thought out loud. "And it sounds like Ophelia's past friends and employers are closing ranks to protect her."

"I'll keep digging, and maybe the police will come up with some information that I can't have access to. But I think our best way of finding information is to snoop and ask the suspects questions directly." Kate glanced at her watch as she spoke and gave a quick gasp at the time. "I'm going to be late for another appointment if I don't get moving. Let me know if anything develops, and I'll pump some of my contacts harder."

"And while you're doing that, I'm going to ask some questions. Starting with Tiffany."

Kate paused with her hand on the doorknob and turned back to Lizzie. "Just remember, one of them is a killer," she warned.

LIZZIE HAD LITTLE TIME to think about Kate's warning as the morning sped by.

She'd spent the next hour working with Piper on her ideas for setting up the next segment. Piper wasn't a disappointment, and Lizzie wished her friend could stick around longer than the emergency relief she was giving. Between her and Trisha, they seemed to feed off of each other, coming up with plenty of new ideas, some a little out there but workable. As Lizzie had chimed in with her own thoughts, Kevin had stood back and watched the trio in awe. Lizzie noticed his expression and walked away from her two friends to stand next to Kevin. She reached out and squeezed his hand and gave him an encouraging smile.

"Don't worry, the three of us are like this all the time when we get together, and if we add Megan to the mix, it's even worse. But I think we've come up with some good ideas that Trisha and you can implement in upcoming segments. Trisha will be able to run with them and bring everything to fruition."

"All I can say is I'm glad this doesn't happen too often. I'd never keep up with it." Kevin gave her a hug, and the two of them laughed. Lizzie leaned against him for a moment and reflected she was lucky to have such good friends.

"I think you guys have everything under control here. I'm heading back to the office to get some paperwork done," Kevin said.

"You're right, I'm not needed here right now, either. I am going to find Tiffany and see if I can probe a little into her past."

"You're only asking discrete questions, remember? Richard's orders. As well as my concerns. I don't want to be worrying about you." Kevin paused before he walked away and turned back and gave her a quick kiss, along with his warning.

"I promise I'll be discreet. Who knows, maybe I'll have it all solved by the time you come back." She laughed.

Kevin shook his head and pushed the hair out of her eyes. "Just be careful, Lizzie."

Lizzie saw his concern and gave a nod, and then looked around to see where the film crew were working. Luck was in her favor. Tiffany was standing away from the others, working on her computer. This was the perfect opportunity, and Lizzie wasn't about to let it go by.

"IT MUST GIVE YOU AN inordinate amount of satisfaction to not only renovate the gardens but also to bring this old house back to life."

Tiffany and Lizzie had been talking about flowers and plants for the last five minutes, with Harry busy chasing the many butterflies inspecting the flowers for pollen. It soon became clear to Lizzie that Tiffany had a working knowledge of horticulture. She also was hearing a slight dialect accent as Tiffany expressed her enthusiasm for plants.

Lizzie tested it out a bit more and pointed out a few plants that were more tropical. Sure enough, Tiffany knew just what they were. And they were obscure enough that only somebody who lived in the South would know them. It was when Tiffany easily identified the black bat flower that Lizzie connected the dialect and the horticulture knowledge. Tiffany's knowledge about the black bat was a clear sign she came from the southern swamp areas of Louisiana where the plant was native. It was just an odd coincidence that Lizzie had found it on her property, probably brought in by some long ago relative who had visited the bayou areas and wanted to bring a touch of it to Florida.

If it had only been her horticulture knowledge, Lizzie might have put it down to a coincidence, but the more she talked, the more Lizzie could hear the touch of New Orleans in her voice.

"What parish are you from? " Lizzie asked, taking Tiffany by total surprise.

"St. Martin." the woman responded without thinking, giving her secret away.

All along, Tiffany had been telling everyone that she was from the high-end area of Palm Beach. Granted, there were some affluent areas in the parish of Biloxi where she came from, but there was something that told Lizzie the younger woman was more from the backwaters than from the high society of Louisiana.

Lizzie gave the woman an encouraging smile, hoping she would continue to provide more information. But Tiffany was so flustered at letting out her secret that she made some hurried excuse and left Lizzie standing by herself, watching the young woman hurry over to where Ophelia and Tony were working.

"Well, Harry, that is an interesting development. I wonder why she's trying to hide where she really is from. And what else is she hiding?"

Lizzie picked Harry up as she spoke and smiled when he meowed in response. "Too bad I don't talk cat. I bet you have all the answers, don't you, my friend?"

Chapter 32

Kevin worked through the afternoon, clearing his desk and in-box of all the miscellaneous work he'd been putting aside. As he signed the last paper, he leaned back in his chair with a satisfied sigh and reflected on how much he could get done without the chattering of Trisha and Emma in the background.

It wasn't as if they distracted him on purpose or that they were just spending the time talking. No, those two were always full of ideas, and Kevin was their convenient sounding board. And he had to admit to himself, 90 percent of the ideas the two of them came up with were fantastic. It was just a little exhausting trying to keep up with them all the time.

Kevin liked the slower pace of being with Lizzie. She didn't need a sounding board; she thought things through on her own, decided, and then talked about them.

As he thought of Lizzie, his smile broadened. Kevin was determined to take their relationship to the next level. He had been putting it off for too long, letting her push him aside for the day-to-day activities they both had. They'd been best friends, convenient dates, and each other's plus-one for too long. Now that Lizzie was retired, and even if she went back to college to help, it was time for the two of them to spend more personal time together and see where it led to.

While Kevin was having these soul-searching thoughts, the door to his office opened, and Detective Richard Mendoza peeked his head in.

"Hey, Kevin. I knocked, but no one answered. Hope you don't mind me making my way in. It's unusual for it to be so quiet around here, isn't it?"

"A bit, and I have to admit, it was kinda nice. But I think it would get old fast, working on my own. Take a seat. Relax for a minute. You look worried about something."

Richard walked over to the soft chair in front of Kevin's desk and dropped himself into it, letting out an exasperated sigh as he did. Nothing was said for a few moments as he gathered his thoughts, but Kevin could tell something was bothering him. Finally, he couldn't stand it any longer.

"What's up?" Kevin leaned forward, urging his friend to speak up.

Richard ran his hands through his hair before he spoke.

"We did some more background digging on our two murder victims, and you're not gonna believe what we found out."

"Earl was definitely murdered?"

"It wasn't suicide, unless he could miraculously hit himself on the back of the head hard enough to crack his skull, causing instant death."

"Geez, that would take some brute strength, wouldn't it?"

"Either that or a lot of anger and just the right angle. We can't rule out either."

"So, what did you find out that's got you so perplexed?" Kevin asked, getting back to Richard's original statement.

"You know how everyone went out of their way to tell us that Earl was a groupie, always following Camille from job to job?" Richard shook his head as if still in bewilderment and then leaned back into the chair to make himself more comfortable.

"Yeah, that seemed to be the general consensus."

"Well, it seems the two of them had more history than that. Earl was Camille's ex-husband."

"What!"

"Yeah, that's pretty much how I reacted too," Richard grinned at Kevin.

"You think that's why he had her phone?"

"You mean like she might have given it to him for safekeeping? It's a possibility," Richard mused.

But Kevin was shaking his head even as he spoke the words, knowing full well Camille would never have given her phone to Earl—ex-husband or not.

"No, it makes little sense. Camille's not the type to have given up anything that belonged to her, regardless of who it was and what the relationship was to her."

Richard nodded, agreeing with Kevin's assessment. "I would bet he saw an opportunity to take the phone, probably after she was found dead. And maybe even found her notes about her employees."

Richard and Kevin exchanged looks, each thinking the same thing. Someone knew Earl had the phone.

The two men were silent, each wondering what this new piece of evidence could mean. Did it have anything to do with Camille's murder or was it just a coincidence?

"So, did you let anybody else know about Earl's relationship with Camille?" Kevin asked.

"No, I will not make a general announcement about it. I was just going to let you know, and I figured you'd let Lizzie know. Let's see where her questions lead after she has this information. I'm getting nowhere with the suspects. At this point, they're not even answering my questions. I hope Lizzie has better luck." Richard slapped his hands on his lap and got to his feet. "I got an interesting phone call from that reporter, Kate. She asked if Tony was in witness protection. Not that I could tell her anything, but it's given me a new angle to look at, so I'm off to get more information on him."

"Yeah, Kate seemed pretty perplexed about Tony. But then again, she's not getting anywhere with the other two suspects either. By the way, Kelly is going to stay with Lizzie for as long as she needs, even after you wrap up this investigation, if she wants." Kevin also got to his feet and walked his friend to the door. Richard acknowledged his words with a nod, and they shook hands. Moments later, Kevin heard the outer door to his office close, and the silence afterwards seemed to engulf him.

"I've done enough work here today. Something tells me I need to be back at the plantation," he mumbled to himself, his voice echoing in the empty office.

Chapter 33

Lizzie found no opportunity to talk to either Tony or Ophelia. It seemed Tiffany had warned them off about her questions. She watched as the three of them closed rank and worked in close proximity of each other for the next several hours.

It was Piper who unintentionally came to her rescue.

"One last thing and then we'll take a lunch break," Piper called out to the crew. They turned their attention to her, and Lizzie hid her smile as she saw Tony rubbing his stomach. It appears the film crew had gotten used to the chef's cooking and were looking forward to their lunch break.

"We've agreed to do a small segment of the episode out by the remains of the old gazebo. But I don't want it to look so rundown. I want it to look like it has the potential to be something grand. So, my friends, that means we need to take out a few chairs and a small table. I want to set it up so it looks like afternoon tea could be set there."

"That's a great idea, maybe we can get Harry to pose in the picture too," laughed Kelly, who was trying to untangle some wires, but Harry's help was making it difficult.

"You never know with Harry. Tony why don't you and I work on taking the Adirondack chairs over?" Lizzie hurriedly butted in before Piper could assign her tasks. This was a perfect opportunity to pull Tony away from the others. Piper shot her an inquiring look and then gave Lizzie a nod when she realized what was going on.

"That would be great. Tiffany, can you go to the main house and ask Nora for a fancy tablecloth and a tea set and some cups? And Ophelia, I'm sure if you were to ask sweetly, you could get Josh to give up some flowers from the greenhouse to add to our setting." The two women nodded, and then Piper instructed Emma and Kelly to work on finding a low table that would be proportional to the Adirondack chairs. "There are plenty of tables over on the porch at the main house. We'll get this all set up, and then we'll take our lunch break. By then, the sun will be in just the right position for the gazebo shot."

Piper had effectively separated all the players. It was now up to Lizzie to extract as much information from each one as she could before they got back to filming.

"Come on, Tony, they're not really that heavy, but it definitely will take the two of us to carry them. They're so bulky." Calling out to Tony, Lizzie motioned to the two chairs that were set up by the fireplace. Tony made a motion of flexing his muscles, causing the girls to giggle, and then walked over to grab a side of the chair to help Lizzie. That was the signal for everybody to head out and do their assigned task, the promise of lunch discouraging any dawdling.

As everyone went their separate ways, each intent with the job ahead of them, Harry looked around, watching their activities almost as if he was trying to decide who to follow. Then he got to his feet, swishing his tail and meandered over to stand in front of Lizzie and Tony. With one swift motion, he jumped up and tucked himself into the Adirondack chair they were getting ready to move. Harry's action was just the mood breaker Lizzie needed. As she and Tony shared a laugh, it seemed to put the younger man at ease.

"This is some place you got here, Lizzie. I bet in its heyday it was amazing."

"It was, but I think it's pretty amazing right now as well. But I know what you mean. There used to be sprawling acres of cattle and agriculture. The area is well known for horseracing and breeding."

"Yeah, I come from some pretty impressive houses too, but more city rich than country rich if you know what I mean," Tony bragged.

"I've never been one for the city. But I've visited some beautiful homes. And of course, nothing beats the mansions along the rivers up north, just outside of New York City."

"Yeah, my family's not into mansions. They're more into the high-rise lifestyle, and that can get pretty expensive. Plus, it's a lot easier to do business from within the city for my family."

Lizzie was silent for a moment as she digested the information. Tony's bragging given her answers about his background that she wouldn't have been able get with direct questions. She gave him another opportunity to brag.

"Family business is definitely important, whether it be farming or manufacturing. I think the family that works together has a better chance of success."

"Ha—my family is not into agriculture. Most of them wouldn't know how to handle a shovel." Tony laughed, "Myself included. Yep, it's city-dealings for us. And there's a lot more opportunity to expand when your family runs the city."

"You come from a large family, then? That must have been nice growing up. It was only me and my cousin Freddie. There were a lot of times I wished for a more extended family."

"Yeah, be careful what you wish for, Lizzie. The more family that gets involved, the more problems that arise. That's why I'm here, not back home. Trying to avoid family problems." Tony's voice trailed off as he finished speaking, and the two of them were silent for a moment. They concentrated on putting the chair in position and then straightened up, ready to head back to get the other one. Tony laughed when Harry jumped out of the chair and led the way back to the last chair.

"That's some cat you got."

"That's true. There's only one Harry."

They repeated the process with Harry jumping up on the chair and being carried across the lawn, but Tony didn't speak any further about his family, and Lizzie felt it best to drop the subject. But she asked one last question before they headed toward the house.

"Don't you miss not getting a Chicago pizza around here?"

"Why would I want a Chicago pizza? It's a New York pizza for me. That's the only kind worth eating." Lizzie joined his laughter and nodded at Tony. He didn't realize it, but he just told her what city he was from.

When they arrived at the bed-and-breakfast, Lizzie wasn't at all surprised to see her cousin Freddie hanging around. She quickly introduced Tony to Freddie, figuring the two of them would entertain each other. At the very least, they would try to out brag each other and that would keep them occupied. Looking around, she noticed everybody was back from their assignments except for Ophelia.

"I hope Josh hasn't gone crazy and given Ophelia more flowers than she needs. You all will start your lunch. I'm going to go see if I can rescue her. Josh loves to share his flowers, and I don't think Ophelia will say no to him."

"But don't take too long and tell Josh to come over for lunch too." Nora handed Lizzie an apple to eat on her way over to the greenhouse with her instructions. Lizzie smiled her thanks and then, before anybody could dissuade her, hurried out the kitchen door and headed across the gardens toward the greenhouse.

Chapter 34

Emma frowned as she watched Freddie speaking to Tony. She didn't like the fact that he was hanging around so much or the frequent glances he kept shooting at Kelly. When Freddie and Tony separated, Emma narrowed her eyes as she watched Lizzie's cousin stare toward where they had just come from.

"There's another table that might work better. Maybe we ought to take it out after lunch." Kelly's voice broke into Emma's thoughts, and she turned her attention to the younger girl, pointing to a hidden table just outside the kitchen.

"You're right, that is a much better table. We'll finish early and exchange tables. But right now, I'm hungry." Emma pushed the thoughts of Freddie away and linked arms with Kelly, leading the way to the dining room where the chef had set out a beautiful lunch for them, as well as the guests of Azalea Plantation.

Emma urged Kelly to eat quickly so they could exchange the table and prepare the setting for filming. She like to be on top of things and appreciated that Trisha and Kevin had put so much trust in her as she was winding up her internship. Finishing up, the two of them rushed out the door of the kitchen.

"Nora won't mind if we take this stuff off it and will place by the door. We'll put everything back like we found it after the shoot," Emma pointed to the house plants sitting on the table as she gave her instructions to Kelly. A few minutes later, the two of them, each holding a side of the table, were walking across the lawn toward Lizzie's house. They skirted around the front of the house, making a wide path to the backyard where the old gazebo was settled in the far corner closest to the stream that led into the pond. They placed the table in the center, more toward the back, so the film crew would have plenty of room to move around. Emma stood back and inspected her work, noting that the gazebo had the feeling of being ready to fall on its side at any moment.

"Pipers got the right idea, but I hope the structure will hold up with all of our movements."

"It looks like it's been here as long as Lizzie's house." Kelly answered.

"Maybe not that long, but certainly it's been here for a while. I know she has plans to rebuild it back to its original look. I believe that's on the schedule for after the gardens around the main house are completed."

Kelly nodded and looked around her. It was a beautiful spot, and she could understand why Lizzie would want to refurbish it. The stream was wide enough you couldn't just jump it but would be easy enough to cross if there was a small wooden bridge. It seemed to move pretty swiftly as it emptied into the pond and as she watched, Kelly couldn't help noticing the abundance of wild birds in the area.

"I can imagine how amazing this place will look once the gazebo is fixed up. It's perfect for sneaking out with a book and picnic to play hooky."

Emma chuckled at Kelly's suggestion. It was the same thing she had been thinking.

"Speaking of books, I've got one I think you'll enjoy. We have a few moments before the others get here. Let's run upstairs and see if I can find it. I left it in the reading area with Lizzie's books."

Kelly agreed to Emma's suggestion, and the two of them hurried off to the back door of Lizzie's home.

"You're right, this book looks great. You sure you don't mind me borrowing it?" Kelly turned the book over to read the back cover, smiling. It had taken Emma a few seconds to locate the book once they had entered the mezzanine. Lizzie had been working on organizing the books, and it wasn't where Emma remembered.

"Don't worry about returning it. I've already read it, and I'd rather pass a book on than keep it collecting dust." Emma waved Kelly's question off as she looked out the window and then frowned as she saw the figure of a man walking around the fireplace on the patio.

"I swear that's Freddie. Wonder what he's up to now? Lizzie wouldn't be happy to know he's wandering around her home when she's not around."

Kelly walked over to stand next to Emma, sighed, and looked out the window. "You're right. Maybe we should go downstairs and discourage him."

Emma nodded in agreement, and the two of them turned and rushed down the stairs, clumping on the hardwood. But by the time they had reached the back kitchen door that led out onto the patio, there was no sign of Freddie.

Emma looked around, wondering what he'd been up to. It took a few moments before she saw his work.

"I know those cords were all straightened out so that nobody would trip, and it would be easy to wind up the equipment. Now look at them!" Emma pointed to the extension cords that were now all tangled and wound around some of the equipment.

"Why would he do that?"

"Spite, pure and simple. I think Freddie loves to make things difficult for Lizzie. I've seen stuff like this before. He's got a jealous streak in him that has turned malicious." Emma paused and looked toward the main house, but Freddie had disappeared, and she wondered where he was. Probably up to no good.

"Come on, Kelly, we have a few minutes. Let's hurry and straighten this out and look around to see if there's anything else out of place." Emma picked up the first cord near the chair and started unraveling.

Kelly followed her lead, and in no time, they had undone the tangled mess Freddie had created. When they had finished with the cords, they separated, and each took a side of the of the area to inspect for any other problems. But there was none to be found.

"He didn't have enough time to do any more. I hate to burden Lizzie with this. She's got enough to do with dealing with Camille's murder and a new film crew. You know what? I think you and I can handle Freddie. We'll keep an eye on him, and when we catch him in the act, confront him." Emma stood with her hands on her hips, looking down at the now perfectly laid out extension cords and lined-up equipment. There was no reason to let anybody know the trouble Freddie had caused. But Emma was going to keep her eyes on Freddie, and if she was honest, she was rather looking forward to confronting the meddlesome man.

Chapter 35

While Emma had been watching Freddie's movements, Lizzie had been watching her three suspects. Considering that there had been a murder on the shoot, she was amazed at what their demeanor was. They weren't exactly carefree, but they were definitely at ease. They didn't seem to be troubled by what was going on. Lizzie wondered how much that would change when they discovered Earl had also been murdered. Two of them would be astonished. One of them already knew and was very good at covering up his or her reaction.

Lizzie wanted to question all three of them before word got out about Earl's demise. She had two down and one to go and, so far, was no clearer on who the murderer might be.

The three of them, Tiffany, Tony, and Ophelia, were talking amongst themselves as they waited for Trisha and Piper to provide direction for the afternoon shoot. Not one of them was sending uneasy vibes, and to a casual observer, it would seem as if nothing was amiss. Lizzie glanced at her watch and knew Piper would arrive at any second. She looked down the driveway, searching for any incoming vehicle, wondering what was keeping Kevin. He promised to be here when his office work was done.

"I hope he didn't get tied up with something. I'd really like him to be here when I tell them all about Earl's murder." Muttering, she turned her attention to what was becoming a well-worn path from the plantation house to her home and watched Piper and Trisha approach.

"I am going to have to create a pathway and some gardens between these two houses before the lawn is ruined." She thought to herself, "If I curve them in just the right way and plant a few Crape Myrtle and Gardenias, it will also give me some privacy from the bed-and-breakfast guests."

"I can see the wheels turning; she is planning something." Trisha made the motions of wheels turning, as she motioned to Lizzie.

"I remember that look, and it always meant extra work for somebody." Piper joined Trisha's laughter as they reached Lizzie.

"What's so funny?" Lizzie looked at them inquiringly, but they only chuckled.

"Let's finish getting the gazebo set up," Trisha ignored Lizzie's question and pointed toward the gazebo.

"Where's Ophelia with those flowers? Josh promised they'd be ready after lunch, and all she had to do was pop in and grab them?" Piper asked.

"I'll run over to the greenhouse and see if she needs any help. Knowing Josh, he distracted her when she went to pick them up. They really hit it off with their love of southern flowers." Lizzie saw an opportunity to get Ophelia by herself to ask some questions, and she grabbed it. There had been no opportunity before lunch with Josh walking back for lunch with her and Ophelia. Without waiting to see if her two friends would object, she hurried off toward the greenhouse once again, leaving them to deal with getting the gazebo ready for filming.

Lizzie caught up with Ophelia just as she was coming out of the cutting room of the greenhouse. Her arms were laden with bright-colored flowers and sweet-smelling jasmine vine that could be wrapped around the frame of the gazebo that was still standing. Lizzie rush forward to help the other woman who was struggling under the amount of plants she was carrying.

"I had a feeling this would happen. Josh always goes overboard. He's so proud of his flowers and more than willing to share them." Reaching out, Lizzie took a bundle of flowers from Ophelia's hands, hoping to lessen her load. Ophelia smiled back at her, shaking her head.

"I rather think it was my fault. Everything was so beautiful in there, and it seemed like everything I looked at was more attractive than the last. I couldn't decide. Josh was so helpful, and he offered to help me carry stuff over. I guess I underestimated how much I had. Here, take this pile before I drop it." Olivia shifted a few more bundles of flowers into Lizzie's hand, smiling appreciatively.

"I completely understand. I have the same problem when I go to pick up flowers to put on the tables at the bed-and-breakfast. It's gotten to where I don't even do it anymore. I leave it up to Josh to send over what's currently at its peak for the guests to enjoy."

"He sure has a fantastic job. I can't imagine being surrounded with such beauty day in and day out, not to talk about all the wonderful scents." Olivia lowered her head into a bouquet and sniffed appreciatively, proving her point.

Lizzie smiled at the other woman's lowered head and realized she had just been given the perfect opportunity to start her questioning.

"You're so right. I loved leaving the office at the college and coming out here to inspect what was going on in the labs. It was my favorite part of the day. You must've had some interesting jobs. You haven't always worked in film, have you?"

This is my first job in the film industry. I've always done more small office work, usually charitable–" and she stopped, cutting herself off before she could say anything more. Lizzie looked at her and saw the nervousness Ophelia suddenly had. She clearly had not wanted to let it out that she'd work for a charity organization.

"I've worked on the board of charity organizations myself. It can be quite a challenge, and I admire anybody that can deal with all the input from both the donors and the organization."

As Libby said the word donor, the color washed from Ophelia's face, and Lizzie had an inkling of what the problem had been.

"There is always that donor that wants to remain anonymous, and then you have to figure out how to put the money into the system and keep their anonymity. I used to think it would be just easier if they hadn't donated at all, just thrown the money in a pot and walked away."

Ophelia gulped and looked away from Lizzie's inquiring eyes for a moment, then she straightened her shoulders and looked back.

"You're right. It is a challenge to keep track of the money coming and going, and sometimes misunderstandings happen. But I've always rectified any kind of misunderstanding."

Lizzie slowly nodded, understanding the meaning behind Ophelia's words. Then she changed the subject, not wanting to make the other woman nervous.

"Well, with all these flowers, we should be able to make that gazebo look like it's in perfect shape. We can use the vines to camouflage the gaps in the wood and hide the rot down at the bottom with some of these bouquets. Piper had an excellent idea."

Lizzie could see Ophelia's visible relief as she let out her breath, clearly relieved that Lizzie would not pursue questions about her previous job any further. Her smile became more genuine, and she and Lizzie headed to the gazebo to finish the task at hand.

IT TOOK LITTLE TIME for them to decorate the gazebo. Nora had sent out a beautiful tea tray filled with old English porcelain cups and a teapot and a hand embroidered tablecloth to lay across the table Emma and Kelly had brought over. Piper and Tiffany got to work stringing up the flowers to the gazebo with some fishing line that Piper had brought with her. In no time, it looked like a spring setting, there were enough flowers left over to make a bouquet of birds of paradise, philodendron leaves, and ginger and place it on the arm of one chair. Stepping back, Piper gave a nod of approval and then started giving directions to the crew to film.

"Lizzie, I just need you to sit in the chair and look like a hostess. We'll film this part and take some still shots before adding it to a question-and-answer segment."

Trisha stepped up to fuss with Lizzie's hair, and then Lizzie followed Piper's directions and sat in the chair. Piper then directed Tony to film a few quick shots of Lizzie surrounded by the tropical flowers and then concentrate on the architecture of the gazebo and the stream in the background.

"The idea is to give the audience the sense of what is going to come of this gazebo. As well as a vision of the past."

After several takes, Piper and Trisha were both satisfied and gave Tony a thumbs-up signal.

"That's perfect. I can definitely work with that."

"This spot just reeks of romanticism. I can see a woman in a long hoop skirt and a bonnet sitting next to a handsome man in a top hat enjoying their afternoon tea," Trisha added.

As if on cue, Kevin arrived at the gazebo. Lizzie gave him a wave and smiled brightly when she saw him.

Piper nudged Trisha in the ribs and nodded her head to the couple. "I agree. I can picture that as well, or maybe even a modern-day couple..."

Lizzie and Kevin ignored the gentle teasing, and Lizzie looked inquiringly at Kevin. She could tell something was up and wondered what was going on. But she didn't have long to wait. Kevin had taken action, and he made a motion for everybody to gather around.

"I had a visit from Detective Mendoza this afternoon. I'm sorry to tell all of you, but Earl was murdered last night."

There was a collective gasp from those who didn't know this information, and Lizzie was glad she had kept it from them. She searched their faces, watching for their reaction. They all seemed genuinely shocked.

"There's something else, something you're not telling us." She whispered to Kevin as the others talked amongst themselves about the newest development.

"I sure do, and you won't believe it. But we'll talk later when we're alone," he whispered back.

"I think that's enough for today. My condolences to all of you for losing your friend. I think if we start early in the morning, we can wrap this up tomorrow. Then you can go back to your lives."

Trisha took charge, breaking into the muttering voices around her. With Kevin's announcement, there would be no more concentrating on work for the day. The others quickly agreed and dispersed, almost as if they were eager to leave the plantation and thoughts of death behind them.

Emma and Kelly helped clear up the equipment after the others had left while Trisha and Piper grabbed their notebooks and headed over to Piper's room at the B&B to go over their thoughts about the work to be done to finish up the segment. Lizzie and Kevin watched everyone disperse to their own devices.

"What's going on, Kevin?"

"Let's take a walk where there is no listening ears, and I'll let you in on what's going on." Taking her hand in his, Kevin led the way in the opposite direction that everyone else had gone, heading toward the garden paths that led to the greenhouse and some quiet sitting areas where they could talk in private.

Chapter 36

Lizzie and Kevin walked, moving up and down the path until they were sure there was nobody following them or within listening distance. By the time they picked out a bench to sit on, the sun was getting ready to set and an evening breeze was picking up. As the breeze blew, the scent of tropical blossoms and herbs from the nearby gardens mingled together to create a unique blend. The sounds of the large birds from the preserve coming in to nest for the evening could be heard and Lizzie looked around her, spotting one of the large red-tailed hawks that made its home on the plantation and watched as it settled into its nest amongst the swaying Spanish moss.

"Detective Mendoza stopped by my office while I was there." Kevin shifted his position so that he could look directly at Lizzie and waited until he had her attention before he continued. "There's been an interesting development."

Lizzie turned her full attention to Kevin, wondering what more could happen. "Was he able to find out some more background information on our suspects? Because Katie is sure turning up zilch."

"You could say that." Kevin smiled as he anticipated her reaction when he told her the news.

"Okay, so quit stalling and tell me what's going on. What did the detective tell you?"

Kevin sucked in a deep breath, let it out with a whoosh, and answered. As he expected, Lizzie didn't disappoint with her reaction.

"Well, he dropped the news that Earl was more than just a fan of Camille. He was her ex-husband."

"Are you kidding me? That's outrageous. No wonder the poor man followed her around like a puppy dog. She had to have had some sort of hold over him. Personally, if I'd been married to her, and I got divorced, I'd hightail it as far away as I could."

Kevin reached over and plucked a flower petal that had landed in Lizzie's hair before he answered.

"You're probably right. They went out of their way to keep the secret. According to the detective, they have been divorced for several years. You probably hit the nail right on the head. Camille had some sort of hold over him, some secret he didn't want others to know."

"Just like she has secrets about the rest of her staff. And one secret was enough to get her killed." Lizzie leaned forward and put her elbows on her knees, and then rested her chin on her hands. She was looking off toward the greenhouse but wasn't seeing the structure with its elaborate plantings. Instead, she was picturing Camille keeping their secrets, putting information about those she held in the grip of her control with those secrets on her phone.

"Her phone! The detective hasn't told anybody that he has the phone yet, has he?"

"No, he's keeping that information confidential. Why?"

"Because we need to quit playing around. Somebody wants that phone and the information it contains. I'll bet you any money Earl somehow got his hands on it, and that's why he was killed." She hesitated for a moment, thoughts rushing through her head as she went over everything she had learned, which wasn't much, but it was enough to send her in the right direction. "I wonder if Earl discovered what Camille was up to and used the information for his own benefit."

"It would make sense, and it would explain his sudden death. You're scheming. Just how do you think we're going to use that information?"

Lizzie looked at Kevin and slowly grinned. "By working to set our own trap." Jumping to her feet, she pulled Kevin with her and planted a kiss on his cheek in her excitement. Not wanting to lose the opportunity, Kevin grabbed her by the shoulders and stopped her. Looking at her eyes to see if she would squirm away from him, Kevin lowered his head and kissed her on the lips.

"If you're going to do it, Lizzie, do it right." He gently smiled at her as he lifted his head.

Lizzie flushed, but then shook her head and pushed any thoughts of romance out of it.

"Not now, Kevin, we've got to do this, and we need to do it right. We need to text the detective and get this information to our three suspects in a way that will bring them back here to the plantation."

Lizzie sighed, and Kevin agreed with her, then pulled out his phone to text the detective as she instructed. While he did that, Lizzie was sending a personalized message to each of the three suspects, letting them know that Camille's phone had been found and she had it. She asked each of them to come back to the plantation to discuss the information she'd found on the phone.

Kevin looked over her shoulder as she sent the last text and whistled. "You're playing with fire, Lizzie; we need to let your staff know what you have planned so they can stay out of the way and still keep an eye on you and your suspects."

"I know." She paused for a moment, and then slowly, a slight grin appeared on her lips. "I'll be interested to see who responds first to my message."

Kevin gave a slight shake of his head and then put his arm around her shoulders and steered her back toward the B&B.

"First things first, you need an emergency staff meeting—now."

Lizzie didn't bother to answer, she just met his pace, and they hurried toward the main house. As soon as they entered the back door, Lizzie instructed Nora to gather the staff in the back screen room where they met for their breaks. Then she made a brief call to Josh, asking him to join them. She would leave it up to Josh to inform his own employees. She was actually hoping he would send them home if they weren't in the middle of something important. The fewer people on site, the better. Thankfully, there were only a few guests at this time of year, those that were here were off-site doing the tourist stops and attractions, leaving the bed-and-breakfast relatively empty.

Trisha and Piper were the first to arrive. Trisha hadn't left. She was working with Piper and had planned on staying for dinner. Emma and Kelly weren't far behind. While they waited for the rest of the staff to join them, Kevin and Lizzie quickly filled in the others about what was going on.

"Kelly, under no circumstances are you to leave the bed-and-breakfast. You can both spend the night here in my old room. And Emma, you stick by her side." Lizzie's tone and expression prohibited any arguments either of the younger women could have, and Nora moved to stand next to the two women with her hands on her hips.

"They're not leaving this house. There's plenty of room here for everyone."

As she spoke, the rest of the staff made their way into the screen room, and they didn't have long to wait before Josh burst into the room as well. Kevin looked at Lizzie and gave a nod. It was her show now.

"As you know, there's been a murder on the plantation. What you may not know is there's also been one in town that's connected. We and the police believe there are three suspects, and we have devised a plan to get them here and hopefully confess." Lizzie looked at each of her staff, making sure they understood before she continued.

"In order for this to work, I need all of you to stay out of sight. Not only for your safety, but I don't want any distractions that might give the killer an excuse to get away. The police will be here watching everything, so you will not be in any danger." She paused for a moment and took a deep breath. "My number one concern is for you and your safety. If this doesn't work, we'll figure out something else, but I don't want anybody to be here to interfere. We are only bringing the suspects here and trying to trap them with words, not with physical force and weapons. That's what the police are for. Are we clear on all this?"

Those around her looked at her, some with slightly dazed expressions and open mouths not aware of all that had been going on. Others who knew what was going on were nodding vigorously, pleased with a plan that would put this to an end. After a few moments, they talked amongst themselves, and that's when Nora took charge.

"Josh, I think you should send home the rest of your employees. That way we don't have to worry about what's going on over at the greenhouse. Lock it up and then you come over here. Emma and Kelly, I want you to be on hand in case the guests of the plantation come back. We'll need you to keep them entertained and inside the plantation, not wandering off. Maybe we can do some board games and the chef can have some snacks ready for everyone after dinner..." Nora's mind was going a mile a minute as she thought of all that she could do to keep the guests inside the plantation house and out of any danger. Kelly and Emma quickly agreed to her plan, and Josh was out the door before she even finished speaking.

As the back door closed behind Josh, the front door opened, and the last person Lizzie wanted to see walked in. Trisha saw him at the same time and quickly stepped forward to meet him.

"Freddie. You're just the person I want to see." Linking her arm with his, she led him away from the disbursing group coming out of the screen room and took him into the library where the bookshelves were filled with old favorites and new releases. And tucked in amongst those books were the personal photo albums of Lizzie and Freddie's family.

"Freddie, I need your side of the story of the family. It'll be perfect to incorporate some of that into the film segments. You'll help me, won't you?"

Lizzie smothered a grin as she heard Trisha talking to Freddie as they walked away. The man was powerless when Trisha turned on her southern charm and she had it turned on full at this moment.

"Good, Trisha will keep Freddie out of the way. Once he starts talking about the family, she will be able to keep him occupied," Lizzie said as she grinned at Kevin.

"Then all we need to do now is wait and see who responds and who doesn't."

As if on cue, Lizzie's phone signaled a notification, and she looked down to see a message on the screen.

"Tony's our first response. He said he'll be here at the appointed time." She looked around at her friends, "There is no turning back now, the game is afoot."

Chapter 37

Lizzie had deliberately scheduled the three suspects to arrive at half-hour intervals. She figured a fifteen-minute conversation with her would give them plenty of time to leave before the next person showed up. The conversations were going to be short and sweet, and she would not allow for any bargaining.

"I'm going to lay the facts out before them and give them one chance to respond. They'll either deny or threaten, then it's up to you, detective."

The detective nodded his head in agreement. He had arrived a few moments ago and had already dispersed his men to go undercover in search of the different locations around the plantation for surveillance. He wasn't completely sold on Lizzie's plan, but he had learned through experience, sometimes it was easier just to give in and do what she wanted. Besides, Kevin had assured him Lizzie knew what she was doing.

"Are you sure the gazebo is the best place to meet the suspects?" The detective directed his question at Kevin rather than Lizzie, and she glared at him for the snub.

"If Lizzie says that's the best place, I agree with her. Look Richard, it's out in the open. There's no place for any kind of surprise attack from the suspects. We can see them coming and going, and it's close enough to Lizzie's house and the cabins that we can get there quickly. They're not going to show up and talk if they think they're going to be ambushed."

"Actually, there is a spot closer that you can't see from the gazebo. It's on the other side of the bridge leading to the preserve. You remember, don't you Kevin? We had built a fort there when we were kids, but now it's set up for birdwatching. It's perfect, only yards away from the gazebo," Lizzie interrupted Kevin, suddenly thinking of the old fort.

Kevin grinned back at Lizzie and nodded. He remembered the fun times that he'd had as a child, playing in the fort. "And it's big enough that Richard and I could hide and not be noticed. It's a suitable solution, Lizzie. If you didn't know it was there, you would never see it."

Reluctantly, the detective agreed and glanced at his watch. "The wire you're wearing will let us hear any conversation between you and the suspects. We've got about a half hour before our first suspect arrives. Lizzie, are you sure that all the occupants of the plantation are accounted for and are in a safe place?"

"Yes, we've got that handled. All unnecessary staff have been sent home. And there is only one guest staying here. I shuffled him into town with a complementary dinner and theater tickets, so he'll be gone until late this evening. This is the time to do it. We couldn't have asked for an emptier time at the bed-and-breakfast. And Nora is keeping everybody who is here occupied. There should be no interference from our end."

The detective inclined his head in approval, and then added, "And all three suspects have agreed to meet you here at the appointed time?"

"Yes. Tony will arrive first, then Ophelia, and then Tiffany. I have no idea which one of them is guilty, but I have a pretty good idea of what secrets they've been keeping. At least I think I do based on the encrypted messages you gave me from Camille's phone." Lizzie answered the detective with a confident voice, belying the slight uneasiness she had. Before anything else could be said, Trisha and Piper came out to where they were talking in the kitchen.

"Everybody is occupied with something. Even Freddie seems comfortable and not in a mood to cause trouble. Getting him to talk about the family always makes him feel important," Trisha said. "I wish you'd let us help you deal with something, Lizzie. Anything is better than waiting around wondering if you're safe." Piper's worried frown said more than her words, and Lizzie gave both of her friends a warm hug of assurance.

"I'm counting on you to keep everybody under control here. Especially Freddie. If there's trouble to be had, he will cause it. Now quit worrying. This will all be over in a couple of hours, and we can go back to our normal routines."

"You both know I'll be watching out for Lizzie, and Detective Mendoza will have my back. Everything should go smoothly, like Lizzie said, don't worry." Kevin reassured the two women as well, and the detective nodded his head, and then tapped his watch.

"We need to head out to that old fort of yours now, Kevin. We want to be situated and in place before anybody shows up. Lizzie, give us ten minutes before you head to the gazebo."

Lizzie nodded at the detective's directions and smiled reassuringly at Kevin, who was staring at her, his brows puckered with worry. The detective moved toward the door, and Kevin had no choice but to follow. Before he did, he reached out and pulled Lizzie in for a tight hug and kissed her passionately on the lips, not caring who was watching.

"Don't take any unnecessary chances," he whispered as he pulled away.

Lizzie watched the door close behind the two men and then turned back to see Piper and Trisha grinning openly at her.

"Nothing like a bit of danger to bring out the passion and romance, is there?" laughed Piper. Trisha said nothing; her grin said it all, and Lizzie groaned and shook her head.

"Knock it off, you two. We have other things to think about."

"Oh, but we're going to talk about this when it's all over," Trisha piped up with a warning, not letting Lizzie off the hook. Lizzie didn't answer; she just made a shooing motion with her hand to make her friends leave.

Then she walked over to the kitchen counter and opened the junk drawer, the one that every kitchen has. Inside she grabbed the powerful flashlight, a phone a previous guest had left behind that was like Camille's, and on impulse, a small spray can filled with pepper spray. She didn't expect any problems, but it was better to be prepared. She knew she wouldn't be able to handle a weapon, but spraying somebody with the stinging spray would not bother her at all, especially if it meant she was in danger. Looking up at the old-fashioned cat-clock, whose tails swung back and forth denoting the seconds as they passed, Lizzie decided it was time to head toward the gazebo and face the first suspect.

Chapter 38

Surprisingly enough, Tony was on time. Lizzie had half expected him to be running behind. He was so casual about his day-to-day dealings with things on the set, but apparently, he considered his meeting with Lizzie important enough to show up on time. Lizzie watched him swagger across the lawn, whistling casually as if he didn't have a care in the world. But his frequent glances around him belied that nonchalant attitude. When he spied Lizzie sitting in the center of the gazebo, he picked up his pace and hurried toward her.

"Okay, I'm here. You want to tell me why you dragged me out here to talk about Camille's phone?" There was no social greeting, there was no pleasantries. Tony bounded across the final few yards as he walked to the gazebo. Lizzie stiffened at his directness but didn't flinch. "I appreciate that you want to get right to the point, Tony. I have Camille's phone." Lizzie pulled a phone out of her pocket and held it up, not letting him see it closely enough to determine whose it really was and then shoved it back into her pocket. "She's got some pretty encrypted messages about you, and I thought maybe you'd like to talk about it with me."

"And why would I want to do that?"

"Because your real name isn't Tony Poliza, is it? And Camille knew that. How much were you paying her to keep quiet?"

Tony's reaction surprised her. Rather than getting angry, he burst out laughing. "Geez, it never ends, does it? Now you're going to be the one to blackmail me. You better talk to my family; they're the ones paying to keep my name secret. Although I don't think it really makes any difference anymore, I'm tired of hiding." Lizzie looked at him, noticing the nervousness hidden behind laughter. As she stared at his face, she saw a connection that she hadn't noticed before.

"No, I won't blackmail you. I just want the truth. Your family is doing more than hiding you, aren't they? Maybe a little protection from, say, a rival family? What are they involved in? Protection, extortion, drugs?"

"Not drugs. It's one thing my family won't touch. But if you're not in this for the blackmail, then what's going on?"

Lizzie took a deep breath, but she didn't mince her words. "Did you kill Camille? Was the information she had on you that important?"

Tony laughed outright, and snapped the chewing gum he had in his mouth. "Kill her? Not me. As heir to the family business, I don't get my hands dirty doing that kind of stuff. I let her have her little power play in keeping my secret. But only because it suited me. If she had exposed me, it wouldn't have been a big deal. I would've simply gone somewhere else under a new name. It was just convenient to keep up the identity I had already established." He frowned and then mumbled, "I guess we will have to work on something new now."

Lizzie studied his face and saw an open and arrogant expression. Tony was full of himself, sure of his position within his family. Why he was hiding out, she didn't know, nor did she care. That was up to the police to figure out, not her.

"If you weren't worried about Camille letting your secret out, why did you show up here to meet me?"

"Curiosity. I wanted to see how the prim professor would react. Were you going to be dishonest enough to carry on Camille's agenda, or are you so tight laced that you're going to turn me into the cops?"

Lizzie gave a shrug, not committing herself either way. "I'm just trying to find the killer. If the cops are on to you, that's not my problem. I'm sure your family will finagle a way out of any charges you might be facing."

Tony laughingly agreed with her, and then nervously looked around him. "Well, you got your answer. I didn't kill Camille, and I don't know who did. I'm out of here. Looks like I'm going to need to make a few phone calls to the family."

Not waiting to see how Lizzie would answer or react, Tony pulled out his phone and turned away from her, hurrying back toward the parking area while talking on his phone. Lizzie watched him walk away and shook her head. She knew full well whatever problems Tony had with the authorities would be taken care of by his family. But he wasn't a killer, she knew that now.

Lizzie glanced at her watch. The meeting with Tony had been short and sweet. But it had also removed him from her suspect list. Glancing over to the bridge over the stream, she half expected to see Kevin and the detective. But they were going to have to sit tight between the appearances of the suspects and be satisfied with listening. If one of them arrived early, they could easily be spotted and ruin Lizzie's plan. Knowing they were watching her, she gave a thumbs-up sign and whispered into the mic of the wire pinned to her chest.

"One down."

As if to answer her, a barn owl hooted from the preserve, and she smiled at the sound. It made her feel less isolated. The wind picked up slightly, and with it came the sound of a car door slamming shut. Tony was leaving. It would be up to the detective if he was picked up for anything else. Lizzie was done with him and ready to face her next suspect.

Chapter 39

As Lizzie waited for the next suspect to arrive, she couldn't help but think of that passionate kiss Kevin had given her before he'd left with the detective. Was it caused by fear for her safety, or were his true feelings finally coming out? One thing was for sure. The kiss had aroused more than a physical reaction from Lizzie. She was reevaluating her relationship with Kevin. She knew she wanted to go to the next level, but she wasn't sure how fast.

"Quit overthinking it and let what will be will be," she scolded herself.

The owl hooted again, as if agreeing with her, and with a jolt, she realized she had spoken out loud, and Kevin and the detective had also heard her.

"Ophelia should be here shortly," she whispered, hoping they would put her first comment down to part of the interrogation process.

The owl hooted again, and Lizzie looked around, trying to pinpoint his location. It was hard not to notice the beauty of the surrounding area. The dusk had created a mystical feel to it as only the old South can. The musty smell of wet soil close to the stream's edge filled her nose as she breathed deeply. Mixed in with the musty soil was the scent of the sweet almond bush. It was an unmistakable aroma, and Lizzie was glad that Josh had talked her into planting some along the borders of the walkways. It was perfect for nights, just like this, with a soft breeze to carry the scent to anyone who was out enjoying the evening.

In the distance, she could hear the traffic from the main road and then the unmistakable crunch of tires on the Chattahoochee driveway leading to her renovation project, her new home. She turned her head in the driver's direction and watched the headlights approach and stop in the parking area that they had designated for the film crew to use.

"She's here." Lizzie said out loud for her own benefit, as well as those listening. Ophelia plodded across the lawn as if she was afraid of turning her ankle in a rut. She didn't have a flashlight with her, but it wasn't completely dark yet, and the moon was rising brightly in the sky, giving illumination to the area.

"She walks as timidly as she talks," Lizzie muttered. It took Ophelia much longer to walk across the lawn than it had taken Tony to stride across. As she approached, Lizzie took in her appearance and noted that Ophelia had changed from the shorts and T-shirt she'd been wearing earlier in the day. She now wore a short dress with a flowing skirt, one hand thrust deeply into the pocket on the side.

"Hello, Ophelia, I'm here at the gazebo. Thank you for coming." the other woman looked up from where she had been watching how she placed her feet and smiled hesitantly when she saw Lizzie sitting in the gazebo.

"I'm not sure why you wanted me to come. I've answered all the questions the police had, but you said you had her phone. How did you end up with Camille's phone?" Lizzie quickly decided that the most efficient way to deal with Ophelia was to be direct and possibly even scare her.

"Shouldn't your question be what I found on the phone rather than how I got it? Isn't that why you're here, Ophelia, to find out what I know?"

"I don't know what you mean. I have nothing to do with Camille's phone."

Lizzie stood up, wanting to have the upper hand and provide a bit of intimidation to the meek woman standing in front of her.

"Do you know what Camille said about you in her phone notes? Let me tell you, there was something written about each of you, and yours was most enlightening."

Lizzie paused, letting her words sink in, and she watched as Ophelia's eyes widened and her lips trembled as if she was ready to cry.

"You can't believe anything Camille ever said. She was a pathetic liar. And she made up stories to hurt people." Ophelia's voice rose in desperation as she pleaded with Lizzie.

"But there must be some truth to it. Or why would she bother? I know she was blackmailing you. What she said about you was money for nothing. She had a thing about song lyrics and used them to describe each one of her crew members. I found yours interesting. Earlier, you told me you had worked for charity organizations. But is that all you did for them is work? Or did you help yourself to the till and take what wasn't yours?"

Ophelia stared at Lizzie, her mouth partly open, tears in the corners of her eyes. "You couldn't possibly know about that. They promised to keep it a secret. Besides, I paid every penny back, and I never borrowed from the charity's coffers again. But Camille found out and used it against me. I was basically working for nothing, paying her to keep her quiet."

Her head dropped, and her shoulders shook with silent tears. After a moment, she straightened her shoulders and looked directly at Lizzie as if waiting for an ultimatum. "So, what are you going to do with this information, Lizzie? Do I have to continue to be in fear of my secrets coming out?"

"I think that all depends on whether you killed Camille. You had ample reason, plenty of time and opportunity, but did you have the heart to do it?"

"No! I would never hurt anybody."

"Not even to save yourself?"

The angry glare that Ophelia gave Lizzie made her take a step back, but then Ophelia seemed to shake herself out of her anger, and rather than advance toward Lizzie, she turned and ran, heading back toward her car. Lizzie stared at her as she retreated, wondering if the other woman had actually been willing to take the step forward and threaten Lizzie. There was a second there when Lizzie thought for sure Ophelia meant her harm. But then the woman seemed to shake it off and ran. Yet Lizzie wondered if somebody had pushed Ophelia hard enough and she was mad enough, would the woman resort to be a physical threat.

"Meow."

Lizzie looked down to find Harry standing at her feet. The fur on his back stood up, and his ears were pressed back against his head. He had obviously sensed the same thing she had about Ophelia.

"Where did you come from, Harry? I thought you were at the house."

Harry meowed again and rubbed against her legs, as if reassuring her he would always be by her side when she needed him.

"This isn't going very well, guys. That's two down, and neither one of them has admitted anything other than what I already knew. Tiffany has to be the killer." Lizzie's frustrated voice spoke into the air for the ears of the two protectors over in the old fort to hear.

Ophelia's quick exit gave Lizzie a few extra minutes, and she sat down in the chair to wait for Tiffany's arrival, wondering what would happen next.

Without waiting for an invitation, Harry jumped up on her lap, making himself comfortable, facing forward as if to offer protection. Lizzie took comfort in his hefty weight on her lap and scratched him behind the ears. She looked over toward the main house and could see the lights on in most of the downstairs rooms. Through the windows, she could see the shadows of her staff and friends wandering around, and she was glad she'd taken the precautions to keep everyone safe. She knew there were police hiding in strategic places around the plantation, but she felt particularly isolated sitting in the middle of the gazebo, like an open target.

"I hope Tiffany confesses, Harry, and we can put this all behind us." She gave a soft giggle. "I guess I'll process? have to talk to Trisha about her hiring process. No more substitute film crews for us. We'll wait for the people we know."

But Harry had no answers, not even a meow. Instead, he left her side and heading back toward the main house, leaving Lizzie to deal with the next suspect.

Chapter 40

Emma had been dealing with the tension building ever since she had watched Lizzie walk out the kitchen door and head toward the gazebo. At first, she put it down to just worrying about Lizzie's safety and the anxiety of a murderer being on the loose. But as the minutes ticked away, Emma noticed another type of tension. A more personal tension, and it took her little time to figure out where it was coming from.

Emma had been warned by both Trisha and Lizzie that Freddie could be a problem. She had watched his interaction with Lizzie and noticed that Nora and Trisha were often a buffer between the two cousins. Nora seemed to have a genuine affection for the young man, whereas Trisha's intervention was more protective and cushioning for Lizzie. But tonight, everybody's attention was on something else, mainly whether Lizzie's plan would work to capture the murderer.

After Trisha had gotten Freddie to talk about the family albums, she seemed to tune him out. She'd heard the stories many times and often was part of them, having grown up with Lizzie and Kevin. And Nora was busy going from group to group, making sure everybody was taken care of. There was plenty of hot tea for calming nerves, and snacks for those who ate away their anxiety. Left to his own devices, Freddie was taking aim at a more vulnerable person who he felt was a threat. And Kelly did not know how to react.

"That belongs to the Higgins family. It's not meant for outsiders."

Freddie snatched a picture from Kelly's hands, leaving the girls staring at him. Kelly quickly apologized and looked upset. She walked away from Freddie, finding a chair almost in a corner where she would be out of the way.

"That was rather nasty," admonished Emma, before she walked over to sit next to her new friend. But Freddie wasn't done. There were other little digs that he had been doing all evening, and they had intensified whenever somebody wasn't looking. It was clear Kelly was a target, almost as if she was a threat to Freddie that he wanted to eliminate. But when Freddie started gossiping about Kelly to anyone he could corner, Emma got fed up and moved forward to confront the sniveling man.

"What's your problem, Freddie? Kelly's here as a guest of Lizzie, and should be treated that way, not the way you're treating her. You know as well as I do Lizzie would never tolerate this, but you're so cowardly, you have to do it behind her back." There was a shocked silence from those around them that had overheard Emma's statement. Most had not been aware of what was going on.

Piper and Trisha both stepped forward to stop the inevitable confrontation, but Emma was like her mother. She would be quiet and passive for only so long, but once she was riled up, that fiery red hair of hers played perfectly with her temperament. Piper put her hand on Emma's shoulder, but Emma shrugged it off. Enough was enough.

"You need to apologize to Kelly. You're so high and mighty on your family heritage, Freddie, but you sure can't live up to it, can you? Where's all that southern hospitality that made the bed-and-breakfast famous?"

"It's okay, Emma, don't start any trouble. I'm fine. I'll just keep out of Freddie's way."

Kelly moved out of Freddie's line of sight and tried to calm Emma down, but it wasn't working. Freddie sputtered and looked at the others in the room who were staring at him, his own fury rising.

How dare these two women, who weren't family and were barely friends of the family, talk to him like this? Someday, I'll be the rightful owner of Azalea Plantation, and the first thing I want to do is get rid of all these so-called friends of hers.

But instead of saying the words out loud, he turned his fury to the room at large. "What's wrong with you people? That young woman is a runaway and there's been a murder here on the plantation. How do you know she wasn't involved? She has no right to be here. Lizzie's crazy, letting some unknown persons make their way into our family home. You mark my words, Kelly Sky is trouble, and the best thing that could happen would be for the state to take her away and put her back in child services."

There was a collective gasp of horror at Freddy's words, and he found himself the subject of disgusted looks and head shakes. Instinctively, he realized he had gone too far. But he couldn't back down now. Everyone's attention was on Freddie, and nobody noticed Kelly burst into tears and sneak out of the room. Trisha had to grab hold of Emma to keep her from advancing on the wretched man. With her fists clenched, Trisha was worried she might land a blow on Freddie's soft chin. It took a little doing, but between Nora and Josh they got everybody to calm down. It wasn't until the chef, Tom, came out with a tray of fresh hot drinks for everybody to soothe their nerves that they noticed Kelly had slipped away.

"Has anyone seen Kelly?"

Nora stood with the last cup of hot chocolate, looking around the room. She had saved the beverage for Kelly, knowing it was her favorite, but the young girl had not come forward to claim it. Now Nora's eyes roamed the room, noting there was no sign of their young charge. Instantly, everybody began looking for Kelly, calling out her name, and Emma threw a disgusted look at Freddy. If he had kept his mouth shut, this wouldn't have happened. It was Josh who noticed the back kitchen door was slightly ajar. Kelly had disappeared into the evening dusk. Before Josh could react, Harry darted through the door as if he was going to find Kelly and keep her safe.

Chapter 41

As the time approached for the third and final and most probable suspect to arrive, Lizzie watched the parking area. Harry had grown bored and wandered off into the dusk, searching for some nocturnal animal that was small enough to amuse him. Lizzie didn't worry about him. Harry was a coward at heart and if a small mouse or lizard turned to attack him, the overweight feline would run off, probably right back to sit at Lizzie's side.

Lizzie was watching the parking area so intently that it took her a moment to notice the sounds of crunching feet crossing her own patio. Frowning, she turned her attention to her house and watched as Tiffany strode forward with angry steps.

It was hard not to miss the anger. Her arms were swinging, and her footsteps weren't those of a woman strolling down Main Street. The look on her face, the tone of her voice, confirmed Lizzie's suspicion.

"What is the meaning of this? How dare you insinuate Camille had something she was trying to blackmail me with? That's what you're trying to do, isn't it? Because that's sure how your message came across."

Lizzie automatically took a step back, putting distance between her and Tiffany, who now stood close. Tiffany crossed her arms and waited, which was a good thing because at least Lizzie knew she had nothing in her hands that she could use as a weapon. Taking a deep breath and straightening her shoulders, Lizzie stood up as tall as she could, but she was still shorter than the imposing figure.

"Why are you so upset, Tiffany? Was Camille on the mark with her innuendos? Next to your name she had the words the *Great Pretender*. And that's what you are, isn't it Tiffany? You're not from some upper-class family with gobs of money and prestige, are you? No, I rather think you're from some Podunk town on the outskirts of the upper crust looking in, wanting to be just like them."

Tiffany sucked in her breath and clenched her fist. But she didn't answer, and Lizzie continued.

"You're always looking in on the people you want to be like, aren't you? Maybe worked for them? That's how it started—you took a little here, took a little there. Until you had enough to create your own persona?" Lizzie took a breath and continued, filling in the blanks as they came to her. "Then you began taking out credit cards and opening accounts under somebody else's name until you had amassed everything you wanted. And when you were satisfied you had enough, you just walked away, came up with the name Tiffany, and started a new life. But Camille found out, didn't she?"

Tiffany looked like she was going to argue or deny Lizzie's accusation. But just as her anger had built up to where she looked like she was going to strike Lizzie, it suddenly dissipated, and her shoulders slumped. Slowly, she nodded, looking out into the darkness.

"How did you find out?"

"It took some guesswork, and I did some research on the area you said you were from. Oddly enough, quite a few families had something to say about a young girl they had employed who was pleasant and outgoing, but always wanted more. You know, not one of them had a bad thing to say about you, just disappointment that you have chosen the path you did."

Tiffany finally looked back at Lizzie, her eyes wet with tears and her lips trembling. "Do you have any idea what it's like to go without even the basics? The other kids at school always had lunch money. I didn't even have a peanut butter and jelly sandwich. And dinners weren't much better. I spent a lot of time going hungry. And niceties? Forget it. I got what the church could give us and what the other folks in town handed to me out of pity. That's no way for a pretty girl to grow up. There's another way I could have gotten money, but I'd rather steal than sell myself. And that's just what I did."

What pity Lizzie had felt quickly disappeared at Tiffany's words. She was a self-serving woman with no care for anyone else, but was she really a murderer? Lizzie was having a hard time believing this possibility.

"I hated Camille, and I hated she knew my secret, but I didn't hate her enough to kill her," Tiffany answered Lizzie's unasked question.

"Then what happened? How was Camille murdered?"

"I don't know. It must have been one of the others. She had something on all of us. Frankly, I don't care either. I'm glad she's gone. And I'm leaving too. There's no reason to stick around here. If you've guessed, that means the police have guessed. It's best I move along. Sorry about your project not getting finished. This could be a pretty cool place when you're finished. Maybe someday I'll come back and see how it all worked out."

Without waiting to see how Lizzie was going to react, Tiffany turned and walked back the way she'd come, at a slower pace and not as angry. But she'll be plenty angry when the police catch her, Lizzie thought to herself. Then she spoke aloud for the benefit of the two men listening in the old fort.

"Well, I have to admit, I thought for sure Tiffany was a killer. But not one of them seemed like a likely person. Did I really miss the mark? Was it somebody completely different from our three suspects?"

Lizzie raised her hands to take the mike off of her chest, but before she could unbutton her shirt, she heard Harry's cry in the distance. It wasn't the victorious sound of a mouse hunt; it was a cry of distress. Without thinking, she turned in the direction his cry had come from and ran toward the sound.

"Something is wrong with Harry," she called out for the benefit of the two men watching, but she didn't wait to see if they were going to follow. Lizzie knew every path, both natural and animal made on the plantation, and she had no fear of wandering around her home. Harry's cry was coming from the direction of the last cabin, the one that Emma had been using.

Picking up her pace, Lizzie arrived breathlessly at the cabin to find two figures standing on the porch staring down at Harry, who was howling crazily. Lizzie's immediate concern was for the cat, and she bent down to make sure he was okay, but there were no visible signs of wounds or distress. She looked up at the two women questioningly, as if they might know what was going on. The sight that greeted her shocked her to her toes.

"Leave the cat alone and come up here slowly."

Lizzie straightened herself, gently shoving Harry away with her foot, not wanting him to be in the way. Then she slowly did what Ophelia commanded, keeping her eye on the gun held in the young woman's hand. When she reached the top of the stairs, she glanced in Kelly's direction, noting the girls' trembling hands and the leaves mingling with her pink hair as if she had been tousled to the ground.

"Ophelia, what's this all about?" Lizzie's voice took on the authoritative tone she had used as a professor when dealing with one of her students. The tone was calm and unthreatening, but also taking charge.

The gun in Ophelia's hand trembled for a moment until she controlled herself, and then she turned her attention to Lizzie. "You had to be nosy, didn't you? You couldn't just let it go that Camille had been murdered and our secrets were dead with her? Now you've made me change my plans. It's a shame. I really like Kelly, but I'm going to need her to make my way out of here safely. Because I'm sure you have cops all over the place. You're a smart woman, Lizzie, but so am I."

Lizzie looked at Kelly and gave her a slight smile, trying to reassure her everything would be okay. Then she turned her attention back to Ophelia.

"Let Kelly go. She's had enough trauma to last a lifetime, and you know what that's like to be down on your luck too, Ophelia. Why would you want to do that to somebody else? Let Kelly go, and I'll make sure you leave Azalea Plantation without being seen. I know every passage in and out of this land, and I will lead you to safety."

Ophelia hesitated and seemed to consider Lizzie's proposal, then she smiled slyly and waved the gun, indicating both women should walk down the stairs. "Why would I give up one hostage when I can have two?"

She giggled with a slight hysteria in her voice, which was more frightening than the gun she held in her hand. Lizzie reached out and grabbed Kelly's hand, squeezing it to calm her visible trembling. As they walked to the last stair, Lizzie looked around and saw no signs of Harry.

Good, she thought, that means I don't have to worry about him being underfoot.

"All right, Lizzie, you know the area so well. Lead the way to the exit and no tricks. The gun is loaded, and I'm an excellent shot. Some of those charity events included hunting, and I got quite a bit of practice in. Not only learning how to convince the rich to give up their money to help others, but also perfecting my aim with a shotgun and a pistol."

"And when I get you to your freedom, you'll let Kelly go?"

"Kelly, yes I'll let her go," Ophelia hesitated and then smiled, sending a chill down Lizzie's back, "but I'm going to keep you around Lizzie for extra insurance." Kelly gasped, but Lizzie just squeezed her hand a little harder and gave a slight shake of her head to warn the girl to be calm and listen to Ophelia's directions.

"I hope you got your walking shoes on. Some of these paths are a little rough," Lizzie advised Ophelia.

"Don't worry about me. I've done plenty of hiking in my time, and I'm not likely to turn an ankle if we're going at a slow steady pace, am I?"

Lizzie didn't answer. She merely gave a nod and then started down the sidewalk from the cottage. After ten quick steps, she took a sharp turn to the left and led the way into the undergrowth. There was no visible path, but Lizzie knew her way, remembering how when she was a kid she had wandered around the plantation, learning every inch of the land.

The path twisted and turned, and to someone who wasn't familiar with the area, it would be easy to lose all sense of direction. And that's what she was hoping for. After a reasonable length of time, she glanced back at Kelly to see how the younger girl was doing. Kelly surprised her with a slight smile and a nod. It was obvious Kelly was getting her second wind, and a brave one at that. Looking farther back, Lizzie was pleased to see Ophelia was looking frazzled, and she kept looking up to the sky as if trying to see where the moon was for direction. But the clouds had been pushed in by the breeze, and the thick foliage overhead completed the job of hiding any astronomical locators.

When they had passed the same trees for the third time, Lizzie heard Kelly snicker and then quickly cough to hide it. Thankfully, Ophelia was not as observant. The path they were on straightened out, and she led them into an open area. They were now on the other side of Lizzie's house. Her wanderings taking them into the preserve and then back onto her own land at a point where the creek dried up to a mere trickle thanks to the help of some industrious beavers that lived on the land.

Where they came out of the preserve, the house was not visible, but Ophelia was flustered and irritated at the time they had been wandering in the underbrush. Now Lizzie had to figure out a way to use this to her advantage. Ophelia was smart, and as she looked around her, her anger became clear as she found herself in unfamiliar territory.

"I don't know what game you're playing, Lizzie. Are you deliberately turning me around? I don't see any kind of exit from your property. Maybe if I shoot your little friend, you'll be motivated to get me out of here."

To prove her point, Ophelia raised the gun and pointed it at Kelly. Whether she would pull the trigger was anybody's guess, but she never had the opportunity. What happened next was so unexpected and unexplainable that it took considerable talking between Lizzie and Kelly later on to remember it clearly.

As Ophelia took aim with the gun at Kelly, the young girl raised her arm, pointing at something behind her captor. Lizzie followed Kelly's finger, and the sight in front of her had to have been a trick of the moon or delirium. But Harry howled, making it all very real.

At the sound of Harry's ear-piercing howl, Ophelia turned around to see what was going on. She screamed and tried to run, but Harry ran forward, tripping her, sending her sprawling in one direction while the gun went in the other. As Lizzie raced to pick up the gun, Ophelia screamed once more, and Kelly whispered softly "Thank you, Elizabeth Higgins. Ghost or not, your timing is appreciated."

Lizzie walked over and put her arm around Kelly, still pointing the gun held in her other hand at Ophelia. "You saw her too? It makes you a pretty exceptional person, Kelly."

Lizzie looked up from Kelly over to where the shimmering form of her ancestor stood watching them. "You always look after family, don't you Elizabeth? Thank you." Lizzie said the words softly and then raised her voice to a more normal level and spoke into the mic still pinned to her chest.

"You can send in the cavalry, we're in the East area of the preserve, Kevin."

Chapter 42

Kevin looked around the gazebo and smiled. Everything was perfectly in place, and he sent a thankful message to Nora Meadows, asking for help. She had created the perfect romantic scene. The same beautiful tea set that had been used the day before in filming was set on a clean lacy tablecloth, and there was a bouquet of roses arranged artfully by Josh in a mason jar in the center of the table. They were the special roses that he had been hybridizing, the Higgins Rose, and this was officially their first cutting.

The sun was up, but the heat had been intensified enough to make it uncomfortable, yet the slight breeze ruffled the oak leaves overhead, creating a play of light and shadow on the floor of the gazebo.

"I hope everybody follows my instructions and stays away so I can have some time alone with Lizzie," he muttered to himself. Then he looked up and saw Lizzie starting to walk across from her house toward the gazebo, Harry trailing behind her.

"Okay one interaction, not that you could ever control Harry." Kevin laughed out loud and waited for Lizzie.

He couldn't help but notice how calm she seemed, not at all like the night before. She'd been spitting mad over the fact that Ophelia had used Kelly as a hostage, and it had taken quite a bit to calm her down. But eventually they had.

He and the detective had been following Lizzie as best they could as she led Ophelia on the merry chase through the woods of her property. But even he'd been surprised when he got the message through her mic as to where her final destination was. After that everything was a blur, happening quickly.

Ophelia had been handcuffed, and Detective Mendoza had taken her off toward a waiting patrol car. He had also given instructions for the other two suspects to be picked up. There were charges to be brought against them as well, but none as serious as murder. Camille's greed and controlling nature had destroyed a multitude of lives, and even if the others hadn't had a part in killing her, they had wanted too, that much had been clear. Only Ophelia had taken action. And then killed again to protect herself from the information on Camille's phone. Why she hadn't grabbed the phone from Earl after she struck him down hadn't been determined. The detective surmised she had heard or seen someone, and it had caused her to panic and run, leaving the phone still in the man's back pocket.

Nora had immediately taken Kelly under her wing when they had returned to the house, and Emma had been right at her side; partly furious the girl had slipped off, and the other half relieved that she was unharmed. In all the commotion, Freddie had disappeared, which was probably for his own benefit. If Lizzie had been able to get ahold of him after hearing what he had said to Kelly, she probably would've done something she regretted.

"Yeah, Lizzie would've let Freddie have it for once, shame we couldn't see it." Kevin said out loud to himself.

"You're right. Freddie's darn lucky he wasn't around when I found out what had happened." Lizzie had reached his side and heard his muttering. She smiled at the scene around her and then turned back to Kevin.

"Did you do all this?" she asked waving her hand to indicate the gazebo set up.

"Well, I had a little bit of help and a lot of encouragement."

"I bet you did." Lizzie burst out laughing, thinking of the eager hands pushing Kevin to set this up.

"I don't want to talk about Freddie. I want to talk about us. Do you know how afraid I was that something was going to happen to you?" As he spoke, Kevin reached out and pulled Lizzie into a tight hug and then bent down and kissed her. She surprised him by returning the kiss and then stepped back as if she needed breathing room.

"Well, I have to admit it didn't end the way I thought it was going to. I really thought Tiffany was our murderer. How did Ophelia get back here?"

Kevin motioned for Lizzie to take a seat. There was no getting around that they were going to have to discuss it before anything else could be brought up. He gave a sigh and then answered her question.

"She never left. She'd been standing over by the bed-and-breakfast and saw Kelly leave after Freddie's confrontation. It was easy for her to follow the younger girl and take her by surprise. What she hadn't counted on was Harry's interference. Good thing he was there in the end to save you too."

Lizzie gave him a mysterious smile, but she said nothing. She wasn't ready to tell him about the ghostly form of her ancestor she and Kelly had seen the night before. She was still puzzled why Elizabeth had appeared to Kelly when she'd never been seen by anybody outside of the family before, not Kevin, not Trisha, not even Freddie.

"Ophelia was desperate. She was so sure she'd gotten away with everything, and then Earl had phoned her threatening to continue Camille's blackmail scheme."

"Yes, she confessed to Richard how she went to the marketplace, came up behind him, and killed him. She definitely wasn't the sweet little charity worker she pretended to be. We found out this morning that even though she had paid back what she had stolen from one charity, she'd gone ahead and stolen twice as much from another. She had her own little Ponzi scheme working with the charity she worked for, stealing from one to pay the other and going forward. It will be a while before they figure out just how much money she siphoned off of the different charities she was associated with. But that's in Richard's hands, we're done with that now." Kevin cleared his throat and then reached over and took Lizzie's hand. Then with his other hand he reached into his pocket and pulled out a pocketknife.

"What in the world? Please tell me we're not taking another blood oath to become blood buddies again. Didn't we do that once when we were kids?"

"No, I'm going to do something I should have done when we were teenagers." Giving her a secretive smile, Kevin looked upward and stood. Then he walked over to one of the supporting beams of the gazebo and pulled open the pocketknife. Getting down on one knee, he picked a corner of the beam and proceeded to carve in their initials, with a heart sign between them.

As he worked, Lizzie came over to stand next to him, her hand on his shoulder. As he finished the last stroke of the heart, she sat down next to him, and they kissed.

"You're right you should have done that when we were teenagers." She laughed. Kevin gave her a slight push as if they were still youngsters, and Lizzie felt a little off balance. As she straightened herself, she reached out to trace the new initials etched into the wood. And then she saw an old set of initials on the other side of the beam. *EH+JP.*

"EH, Elizabeth Higgins. Elizabeth had a lover." Lizzie whispered in wonderment. She reached out her hand to trace the newly found initials. As she did, she noticed that underneath the beam the foundation had been chipped at.

"Kevin, hand me your pocketknife. There's something underneath all this moss and dirt."

It took several minutes of Lizzie meticulously scratching at the rock to finally break through the little crevice that had been made. Then using the blade of the knife, she slowly widened the gap being careful not to snap Kevin's blade. Kevin's head was bent over hers closely watching her every move. Reaching into his pocket, he grabbed a pen and used it to stuff in the hole and wiggle around. As he brought the pen out, Lizzie gasped.

"There's something in there, Kevin."

They worked even harder, being careful not to let the hole fill back up until they could use the pen to carefully lift the object close enough to the surface for Lizzie to reach out and gently pull it out. She held it in her hands and looked at it and then looked at Kevin.

"Do I dare open it?" she asked.

"I think it was meant to be found right now, so go ahead."

Slowly, so as not to tear the material, Lizzie opened the leather pouch and found inside a small locket. Getting to her feet, she walked over to the table where she could slowly open it and get a good look at what was inside. Kevin leaned over her shoulder, watching and just as curious.

"That's Elizabeth." Lizzie pointed to one side of the open locket where a beautiful woman looked out. The photo was faded with age but was in remarkably good condition. Then Lizzie turned her attention to the other side of the locket and found the picture of a tall man standing next to Elizabeth. It was hard to make out any features, with the age of the photo. But it was easy to recognize the gazebo that they were both standing next to, and in the background was the stream that ran along Lizzie's property.

"I wonder who he was," she whispered.

"It's another mystery for you to solve. Hopefully, it is a lot safer than the last one." Kevin bent down and kissed her lightly, and at the same time reached out and grabbed one of the cookies on the plate. Lizzie laughed along with him and poured tea for the two of them to enjoy. They let all talk of murder and mysteries drop and just sat content to enjoy each other's company and think about where the future would take their relationship.

Chapter 43

Lizzie looked up at Emma, who was standing before them, nervously shifting her weight from one foot to the other. Her hair shone an even darker auburn in the afternoon sunlight beaming through the window as she moved.

"What's on your mind, Emma? Something's bothering you." With a smile, Lizzie's calm voice brought Emma's actions to the attention of everyone else in the room.

They were all gathered in the mezzanine of Lizzie's house, helping her finish putting the books on the shelves. Nora was downstairs fixing coffee, and as Lizzie looked out the window, she could see Josh and one of his crews working in the distance in the kitchen garden. Lizzie looked around her at her friends, Trisha, Kevin, Emma, and Kelly. And there was a recent addition to the friendship; Kate had joined them and was sitting in one of the overstuffed chairs, looking at the surrounding books in amazement.

"And you've read all these books?" she asked Lizzie.

"Of course, I have," Lizzie laughed and then turned her attention back to Emma. "Well, what's up?"

Emma held up her phone and grinned.

"I just got off the phone with my mom. She really wants me to come home. And I think it's time. You guys have been great, but it's time for a new chapter, and I think I have to go back to my roots to begin that."

"Citrus Beach is a nice place to begin again," Trisha answered.

"My work here is really done, and my internship is up at the end of the week, anyway. Besides, I think you have somebody here who would be keen to take my place." She looked pointedly at Kelly, making the younger girl squirm.

"I planned on Kelly becoming part of the team. And we'll be sorry to see you go, but you have to do what you think is best," Kevin told his intern with a smile.

"Okay, well then. I'm going to get packed. Mom sounded like she wanted me to come home as fast as I could. And Piper's already left, so it's time for me to go too."

Emma gave Lizzie, Kevin, and Trisha all a warm embrace and then sped off to the room she was sharing with Kelly to pack her bags. Kelly watched her and then turned to Lizzie, still astonished at what Lizzie had told her earlier.

"I can't believe you're going to let me stay here for as long as I want. A real home."

"It's time you had a proper home. We'll work out all the details, but you're part of the family now."

Kelly followed Emma's example and hugged each of them, saving Lizzie for last. As she gave Lizzie a fierce hug, Kelly heard Lizzie whisper, "Besides the family ghost showed herself to you, and that's all the approval we need."

Kelly giggled as she straightened herself and winked, knowing full well what Lizzie was talking about. Then she raced off after Emma to help her pack, excited about her future as well.

"Well, I'm glad the kid's got a future here. Somehow, the two of you really seem to fit together. And I hope I'll be just as welcome to come and go to watch the changes here at Azalea Plantation." Kate got to her feet as she spoke, indicating she was also leaving. After she had walked down the stairs, Kevin, Trisha, and Lizzie looked at each other.

"Here we are, the Three Musketeers again. What kind of trouble can we get into next?" teased Trisha.

Lizzie was ready to answer when she saw movement, a fluttering of the curtains, and she looked at the mantel and saw an out-of-season azalea blossom. She knew what that meant. Harry's meow confirmed her thoughts.

"I think we need to continue looking for whatever secrets Elizabeth Higgins has been hiding. Whether it's treasure, a secret lover, or some family history that we don't know about, the more we look around her old homestead, the more I'm sure she wants us to know."

Lizzie linked her arms with her two best friends, and the three of them shared a knowing smile.

Don't miss out!

Visit the website below and you can sign up to receive emails whenever Victoria LK Williams publishes a new book. There's no charge and no obligation.

https://books2read.com/r/B-A-VGGF-EVWHC

BOOKS 2 READ

Connecting independent readers to independent writers.

Did you love *Catnip Caper*? Then you should read *Killer Focus*[1] by Victoria LK Williams!

Piper Avery thought her day was bad-then she found the body on the beach!When Piper Avery gets a pink slip, a birthday card, and new neighbors all in the same week, she thinks things can't get any worse. But then she stumbles upon a body on the Florida coastline and her day takes a deadly turn.To add to her troubles, her new neighbors turned out to be none other than her mother and mother-in-law, best friends and full of advice. While Piper is trying to adjust to their presence in her life, she's also juggling the challenges of her photography gallery opening, and the surprise birthday gift of feisty spaniel named Daisy, who proves to be a bit of a diva.Piper has no intention of getting involved in the murder investigation, but when undercover cop Joel Stevenson challenges her, she can't resist. With Daisy by her side, Piper begins to unravel the mystery, even as she's caught up in small-town gossip and drama.As Piper and Joel work together to solve the murder, they stumble on

---

1. https://books2read.com/u/boWOe0

2. https://books2read.com/u/boWOe0

more than they bargained for. With the help of Joel's K-9 partner, Scout, they race against time to catch the killer before Piper becomes the next victim.*Full of humor, mystery, and the beautiful scenery of the Florida coastline, "Mrs. Avery's Adventures: Book 1" is the first in a cozy mystery series that will keep you on the edge of your seat as Piper and Daisy navigate the twists and turns of small-town life, all while trying to keep her nosy mother and mother-in-law out of trouble.*

Read more at https://www.VictoriaLKWilliams.com.

Also by Victoria LK Williams

A Beach House Mystery
Mist at the Beach House
Mist Across the Waves
Mist By The Lighthouse
Mist Across The Sand
Mist From The Sea
Mist in the Cove

Citrus Beach Mysteries
Murder for Neptune's Trident
Scent of a Mystery
Murder at the GeoCache
Runaway for Christmas
Tank Full of Trouble
The Flapper Caper
Borrowed, Blue, Dead
Trouble Has A Tail
Citrus Beach Mystery: Box Set: Books 1,2,3

First In Series Sampler
First In Series Sampler, Volume 1

Hibiscus Cove Cozies
Lost and Hound

Milo's Mysteries
Milo's Christmas Mystery

Mrs. Avery's Adventures
Killer Focus
Final Delivery
The Dummy Did It

Professor Higgins Investigates
Thyme to Depart
Catnip Caper

Sister Station Series
Now Arriving
Now Departing
Sister Station Box Set

Storm Voices
Whispered Voices
Deceptive Voices
Lost Voices
Grinchy Voices

Storm Voices Series Box Set

Tattle-Tale Mystery Novellas
The Toy Puzzle
Her Missing Husband

Standalone
Cozy Christmas Collection

Watch for more at https://www.VictoriaLKWilliams.com.

About the Author

USA Today Best-Selling Author. Victoria writes what she calls ***Cozy Mysteries with a Tropical Twist.*** Her series are set in small South Florida towns, with fun characters and a dog/cat or two. She also has one series that is paranormal cozy and the plans for a second.

Victoria can often be found writing from her South Florida home, looking into her garden, watching the birds and squirrels fight over their next meal, while she writes. Her two cats, Miss Marple, and Fletch, often join her at the desk and each has their assigned spot. Victoria's not sure they are there to supervise her writing or watch the birds.

Victoria and her husband of 38 years share a love of gardening, and together they have written a gardening handbook for Florida gardeners. The Williams are now empty-nesters, giving Victoria plenty of time to dream up the next story.

Until then, you can read any of her current titles in the ***Citrus Beach Mystery*** series, ***Sister Station*** series, ***Storm Voices*** series, ***Mrs. Avery's Adventures*** series, ***Beach House Mysteries, Tattletale Cafe, and now Professor Higgins Investigates.***

Read more at www.victorialkwilliams.com.

About the Publisher

Books by our author, Victoria LK Williams have a tropical twist to them. Her characters are from the south, or are now in the south, but they all share a love of sun, sand & stories!

We are also pleased to offer the book **Pocket Guide to Florida Landscaping**, by *Donald R Williams*.

Ingram Content Group UK Ltd.
Milton Keynes UK
UKHW020657240723
425668UK00014B/721